EDWARD A. GRAINGER'S
CASH LARAMIE & GIDEON MILES SERIES

# THE AXEMAN OF STORYVILLE

## HEATH LOWRANCE

The story herein is a work of fiction. All of the characters, places, and events portrayed in this book are either products of the author's imagination or are used fictitiously.

Cover images from iStock; Design by dMix.

ISBN: 978-0-9912039-6-3

BEAT to a PULP
PO Box 173
Freeville, New York 13068
USA
Email: btapzine@beattoapulp.com
Visit us at www.beattoapulp.com

# New Orleans
# 1921

# One

The killer liked music. He had a phonograph in his room and a stack of long-playing records, and when he had time he enjoyed lying on his cot and listening to them.

King Oliver and Bix Beiderbecke and Jellyroll Morton, they were like prophets, the way they made him feel. Jazz was the reason he'd come back to New Orleans in the first place. It wasn't the same in other cities, not even Chicago or New York.

He especially liked to listen to music before going out on the town with the axe. Jazz put him in the right frame of mind, the right *space*, to cleave someone's skull.

He listened to his records for two hours straight, thankful that Mr. Ventucci didn't start pounding on the wall again and telling him to turn it down. Mr. Ventucci, the local grocer, liked jazz well enough but got annoyed when it went on too long. That was something the killer couldn't understand. If he had his way, the music would be non-stop. The trance would never end.

Finally, he put away the records and got dressed. He knew who he would bless tonight, and she would have started her shift by now.

The grocer he lived behind was on Upperline Street, in the heart of the Italian district. He stepped out into the humid night, clutching his overcoat around his throat. The axe was tucked into his belt under the coat, and the handle rubbed uncomfortably against his thigh and his spine as he walked.

He sweated ferociously, although he didn't feel particularly warm. He caught a trolley to Basin Street resenting the press of humanity all around him, fantasizing about pulling out the axe and slaughtering everyone. A pretty, young girl kept jostling into him, smiling up at him with an apology in her eyes each time, but after the first few times he couldn't bring himself to smile back at her and turned his head away.

He hummed under his breath, just to think of something else. "Weary Blues," the last record he played before heading out. He closed his eyes and tried to imagine he wasn't surrounded by filthy mortals.

At Basin Street, he got out and stood on the corner for a few minutes, just breathing. The tune in his head had gotten louder and louder the whole way, until it was all he could hear. He wiped sweat from his brow and tried to get his heart to beat normally. He tried to find the trance again. It wouldn't do to go to the girl with an unclear mind. It would make using the axe harder.

The District—the area they called Storyville—was crowded and hectic, as usual. All up and down Basin Street and the connecting lanes, red lights gleamed in the dusky dimness. Both whites and Negroes abounded, along with Creoles and Mulattos, men making the rounds from bar to brothel to gambling den and back again. There was a mad cacophony of sound—jazz played in every upstairs window and raucous laughter and yelling rained down on the streets.

He started for Miss Tilly's place, well beyond Basin and the train station, into the seedy heart of the District. All the high-end brothels were on Basin, elegant mansions that didn't betray the depravity that went on inside. The killer had no interest in those places. He wanted Miss Tilly's, that's where he would be closer than ever to The One.

Miss Tilly's was a modest two-story house on the corner of the block, next door (and with an entrance to) a tavern called Shorty Pete's. One of the girls, wearing nothing but an assortment of carefully placed ostrich feathers, let him in, and Miss Tilly herself greeted him in the foyer.

Without looking up and doing his best to remain disregarded, he gave Miss Tilly a wad of bills. Within minutes the killer was upstairs with his sacrifice of choice.

The girl called herself Eva-Lynn. She was a Mulatto girl, about sixteen, with a flat chest and no hips to speak of. But she had a lovely face, clear and innocent as an angel. She looked, like all the others, like The One. Her dark eyes flashed at him. "Take off your coat, handsome. Should I get you a drink?"

He shook his head and started to unbutton his overcoat.

She put a record on the phonograph, something popular from Rudy Vallée. Not one of the killer's favorites, but it would do.

"Hot night for so much clothing," the girl said, sidling up to him. She put a hand on his crotch and rubbed, putting her face close to his. She smelled faintly of lavender and stale sweat.

She started to put her arms around his waist but he moved away from her and took off his coat, being sure to keep the axe at his spine hidden.

Eva-Lynn shrugged and went over to the bed. She dropped onto the pillows and began undoing the straps on her bodice. She spread her legs, stretching lewdly, and said,

"I'm feeling lonely over here, handsome. Come keep me company."

He took a step toward her, and the music seemed to get louder in his head, "Every Moon's a Honeymoon," and his heart started pounding in time to the syncopated beat of it. He felt the arousal beginning, felt the first strains of the damnable clearness, like the entire world was made of glass and he could see deep inside it to the roiling guts of the earth. He could look at the girl and see right into her. There was a core of vile disease in her heart that pulsed black and purple, a sort of cancer in place of a heart. It spread out and out, through her veins, out her fingertips and into the clear glass world.

It was infuriating to witness, it always was, but he maintained the clearness of head by letting the jazz take him body and soul and lift him up into the trance.

Another step toward the whore, and his big right hand, the melody hand, went behind his back and came out with the axe. His left hand, the rhythm hand, gripped the handle and he felt his face threaten to crack under the pressure of a beatific grin and the *purpose*, the beautiful, clear *purpose* came to him.

Eva-Lynn started to sit up, her pretty face going blank with alarm. She looked like she wanted to scream, but couldn't quite fathom that this was happening to her. Her mouth moved and her hands came up in an oddly touching display of beseechment.

He disappeared into the music and, gripping the axe handle in both hands, he swung down, hard, burying the blade in her collarbone.

The force of it slammed her back into the bed. She didn't scream, didn't even groan. The blow had not only broken her collarbone but knocked the wind right out of her.

He yanked the axe out of her shoulder and brought it down again in her face.

And he kept doing it until the record was over.

Breathing hard, he wiped off the axe blade on the bed sheets. Then he started the record over again, his trembling fingers barely able to hold onto the needle.

He slid the axe back through his belt, put on his coat, and left Miss Tilly's place through the window, clambering down to the street below. Two whores coming out of the tavern saw him, stopped cold in their tracks, alarmed.

He started down the street as the whores hurried into Miss Tilly's place.

He wasn't worried. He'd be on the trolley back to Upperline Street before the coppers even stepped foot in the brothel's foyer. Even then, he knew from experience they wouldn't do a damn thing. Who cared about some diseased, morally depraved whore?

In New Orleans' Storyville, they were a dime a dozen.

# Two

"That's it," Gideon Miles said. "I've met my match. I'm a dead man."

Violet said, "No. Say it's not true, Gideon."

"I can't, Vi. I'm done. I'm sorry. This is the end."

He sat at the far back booth of his nightclub, stacks of invoices, bills, and other paperwork spread out on the table in front of him. He looked at it all glumly.

Standing over him, Violet said, "It's just the usual, Mr. Big Shot Club Owner. You need to do it if you want to run this place proper."

He looked up at her. "It's going to kill me, I tell you. How about *you* do it?"

She laughed, leaned over and kissed him on the cheek. "Sorry, baby. You're the brains of this operation. Me, I'm just the pretty face here to get 'em in the door."

He smiled. "Well, you *are* that, all right. What say you and me forget all these bills and go upstairs and—"

"Gideon Miles, get your mind proper on your work, you lewd old man."

She sashayed away, swinging her supple hips just like a girl half her age. Miles watched her walk past the booths and the dance floor and the small stage, into the back rooms. After she was gone, he turned his attention back to the paperwork, the smile on his face fading.

*This*, he thought, *is not what I had in mind*.

He and Violet had opened the VioMiles Club eight months earlier, after settling in New Orleans. They'd spent the previous three years, after Miles got back from France, travelling from West to East and back again, enjoying their new-found leisure and freedom. But there comes a time, Violet said, when a pair of old fogies have to settle down and plant roots.

So that was what they did. Miles bought the old building on Royal Street, not far from Rue St. Louis, and turned it into New Orleans' latest jazz club.

Which was all well-and-good, Miles thought. Except for the goddamn bills and invoices and what-not. As a younger man, he didn't know how he'd spend his old age, but he certainly hadn't counted on filling out forms and writing checks all damn day.

He'd been a U.S. Marshal once, back in the old days, out in what was then called the Wyoming Territory, one of the very first black men ever to hold that distinction. As far as he knew, there had only been one other black man with the Marshals, even now in this new, so-called liberated age.

But being a Negro didn't hinder him in his work. He'd spent years tracking down bad men and bringing them to justice. It was a job he was good at, and by the time he retired, in 1910, he'd brought in more outlaws than just about anyone else on the job, with the possible exception of his good friends Cash Laramie and Bass Reeves.

After retirement, he and Violet got hitched after a courtship that went on for decades. He did some freelance work for the Marshal Service when he felt like it, and in 1914, with the Great War raging in Europe, he went to

France and worked in intelligence until the conflict was over. They treated Negroes differently over there, and he almost stayed. But Violet was homesick, and so back to the States they came.

Now here he was, in New Orleans. A club owner.

He was sitting there, pondering all of this, when a voice at his shoulder said, "Heya, Mr. Miles. Hope I ain't disturbing you, sir."

It was Little Cat Borre, the Creole kid Miles had hired two months ago to help out around the place. About eighteen years old, Little Cat was lithe and good-looking and already a hit with the ladies who came to the VioMiles. Miles had to admit the kid was loaded with charm.

But at the moment, Miles wasn't in the mood for Little Cat's easy smile. He said, "What?"

"There's some ladies in the foyer wants to see you, Mr. Miles, sir."

"Cat, we aren't open right now. And can't you see I'm busy here?"

"Busy staring off into the distance, looks like," Cat said, grinning. Miles started to reprimand the kid for being mouthy, but stopped himself. Little Cat was right, after all.

He sighed, said, "What ladies? What do they want?"

"I don't rightly know, sir. But they's ... um ... not ladies from high society, I can tell ya that much. They come over from the District." Cat wiggled his eyebrows suggestively.

Miles frowned. "Prostitutes? Is that what you're saying? Go tell them we don't need their services here. It's not that sort of club."

"I don't think that's why they here, Mr. Miles, sir."

Miles said, "Oh, for Christ's ... okay, bring them in."

Little Cat nodded and ambled off back to the foyer, and Miles stood up and stretched. *What the hell*, he thought. It was a good excuse to get away from the mind-numbing paperwork, anyway.

The two ladies Cat ushered in weren't dressed like prostitutes, but no one would mistake them for upper crust New Orleans society. They wore drab dresses and no makeup. The older one, a thick-waisted white woman with gleaming auburn hair, said, "Mr. Miles, my name is Miss Tilly. Thank you for seeing me."

Miles nodded, motioned to the booth. "Would you sit, Miss Tilly? May I offer you coffee?"

"No thank you, sir. And we won't stay long enough to sit. But Celissa and I have come to request your assistance."

The younger woman, Celissa, was a lovely Creole girl with dark, sullen eyes and a full mouth. She stood next to Miss Tilly with the sort of arrogance and poise one wouldn't normally associate with a whore.

Puzzled, Miles asked politely, "How can I can be of assistance, Miss Tilly?"

"You've been a topic of interest about town since you arrived, Mr. Miles, and word is that you were once a policeman. Is that true?"

"No, Miss Tilly, not exactly. I was a U.S. Marshal. It's not quite the same thing."

"But you ... well, you found bad men, yes? You tracked down murderers and rapists and all manner of degenerate sorts?"

"That is true. But that was a long time ago."

Miss Tilly clutched her large hands in front of her and looked at him solemnly. "Well, sir ... the skills you acquired in your policeman days—I mean to say, your U.S. Marshal days, beg pardon—are the skills that bring me to you today."

"As I say, ma'am, that was a long time ago. I don't do that sort of work anymore."

The Creole girl, Celissa, smirked. "I told you he wouldn't care, Miss Tilly. Just like everyone else in this awful goddamn city. No one gives a shit about a bunch'a dead whores."

Miles raised an eyebrow at the girl, mildly shocked at the language. It had been many years since he'd had the dubious pleasure of standing before fallen doves, and he'd forgotten how coarse they could be. "It's not that I don't care, young lady. It's just that I don't have an official capacity to assist you. I'm a club owner now. Plain and simple."

"The owner of a jazz club. I hate jazz. I despise it. It brings out the worst in humanity," Celissa said.

"Ignore the girl, please, sir," Miss Tilly said. "Will you … will you hear me out, at least? The police don't care about what befalls us in the District. No one is willing to help, Mr. Miles."

Miles frowned, glancing at the stack of bills and invoices on the table behind him.

He said, "Very well. I'm listening."

Miss Tilly looked relieved, while Celissa huffed and turned her attention to the empty bandstand.

"Last night," the madam said, "one of my girls was murdered, sir. She was attacked with an axe. The killer chopped her up. It was … it was a vicious, monstrous thing to see." She choked up, her wide face going pale.

Miles said, "I'm very sorry. Please, Miss Tilly, won't you change your mind about sitting?"

He motioned to the booth, and the madam nodded very shortly and allowed him to lead her to the seat. She settled in, composing herself, and the girl stood at her shoulder and continued to look around the club with disdain.

When Miss Tilly had regained herself, she continued, "Her name was Eva-Lynn. A sweet, kind-hearted young thing that had only been in my employ for four short weeks. She—"

"—was a bitch," Celissa said. "She thought she was better than the rest of us 'cuz she was all young and fresh-looking."

Miss Tilly glared up at the girl and snapped, "Close your mouth right this instant, Celissa. I won't have you speaking ill of the dead."

Celissa made a dismissive gesture with her hand, walked away to the other side of the club.

Miss Tilly let her go, and turned back to Miles. "Celissa can be a bitter creature sometimes. But Eva-Lynn was a sweetheart. I loved her dearly."

Miles couldn't help himself. "You loved her enough to turn her out for any john with cash."

Miss Tilly went frosty. "I provide a safe haven for my girls. I give them a place to sleep and three square meals a day. And most importantly, I give them a sense of home. Without me, the girls would be on the street or working for some cruel pimp who didn't care about their welfare at all."

Miles nodded, reluctantly. To some degree, Miss Tilly was right. Still, if she cared that deeply about the girls, she would've opened a home for wayward youth instead of a brothel.

But he said, "Please accept my apology, ma'am. Continue."

Miss Tilly sniffed, "The crux of the matter, Mr. Miles, is that Eva-Lynn wasn't the first. Two months ago, another girl was murdered in the District. Not in my house, but close enough. And six months before that, the first. All Creole girls, all young and all quite lovely."

"All with an axe?"

Miss Tilly nodded. "A horrifying way to die. The sight of it is … well, it's something I hope you never have to see."

Miles had seen firsthand the damage an axe could do to a human body; it wasn't something one ever forgot. He said, "And the police refuse to help you?"

"They did nothing when the first two girls in the District were killed. They will do nothing now about Eva-Lynn. I've come here to plead with you, Mr. Miles. Please, sir."

Miles sat back in the booth and studied the woman's face. He pulled a pipe from inside his coat, packed it, and struck a match to it. He sucked smoke for a long moment while Miss Tilly watched him with tears brimming in her eyes.

Finally, he said, "I don't see how I can help you, ma'am. You need a detective. Man-hunting and crime-solving are two different things."

"But we have no one else to turn to."

"Try a private detective. There's a Pinkerton agency here in New Orleans. I'm not the man who can help you."

"But—"

Miles stood up. "That's all I have to say on the matter, Miss Tilly. I'm sorry for your trouble, but there's nothing I can do for you. Good day."

Miss Tilly started to say something else, but Miles had begun walking away from her. At the door to the back rooms, he turned and said, "Little Cat will see you out."

He closed the door behind him, trying hard to ignore the little voice telling him he was a heel and a heartless cad.

*I'm not a lawman anymore*, he told the little voice. *I'm a club owner and a respectable Negro citizen and an old man, goddamnit.*

And that almost shut down the little voice. Almost.

# Three

They had gotten in the habit of taking their evening walk at dusk, when the sun was low in the west and some of the heat from the long day had dissipated. Miles with his expensive derby hat and cane and Violet in her pale summer dress would stroll arm in arm down the length of Royal Street, along Canal and Decatur and all the way back up St. Louis.

A humid wind from the river swept over the rusted iron lattice and ornate stonework of each building in the Quarter, carrying with it the earthy scent of steamed crawfish, oysters, and beer. Music played from every second-story window.

It was a stroll that Miles looked forward to every day, a brief respite before heading back to the club and opening for business at ten sharp. The music would blare then, the bodies would press in upon each other, and the liquor would flow.

Like every other club owner in town, Miles had to pay a fee to the police in order to keep the booze pouring, but it was well worth it. When they'd first opened, Violet had said to him, "Well, well, look at you now. Decades upholding the law, and now you're just a regular ol' low-down criminal, aren't you? Selling illegal booze just like some kind of gangster bootlegger," and Miles had said, "Far as I can recollect, I never did enforce any stupid laws. And prohibition? 'Bout as stupid as a law can get, my love."

She agreed. Hell, it seemed the entire city of New Orleans agreed. The Volstead Act may as well have not existed.

They were on Decatur, with the dark rolling waves of the Mississippi to the right and the wood and stone storefronts, gambling houses, and inns on the left. The streetlights had just popped on, bathing the cobblestoned corners in pale gold light. Violet hadn't spoken in several minutes, which Miles found odd—normally, the woman did love to talk, God bless her, and he'd learned that any extended silence usually boded ill for him.

Just as he was about to break the silence with a weak joke, she said, "Baby ... I was thinking."

"Uh-huh."

"About those ... women ... who visited today."

"Oh Lord. What about them?"

"Don't you take that tone with me, Gideon Miles."

"What tone, Light of My Heart?"

She rolled her eyes, unable to keep from smiling. "Oh, never mind that. I was thinking, though ... well, I wish you'd help them."

He stopped walking, dropped her arm and looked at her. "You're joking."

"Do I look like I'm joking?"

"But I thought you didn't want me doing that sort of work anymore. You hated it when I was a marshal."

"Yes, but ... I feel horrible for them. The police don't care about the ... fallen women in this town, just like Miss Tilly said."

Violet had apparently been eavesdropping on the entire conversation, because Miles hadn't told her every detail of it. He said, "There's nothing I can do to help them, Vi. I'm not a lawman anymore, and I don't have the resources."

"You have plenty of resources. You always have. That brain of yours, that conscience, that sense of duty."

"Maybe, but it's not my duty anymore. I gave all that up."

Violet shook her head. "You never gave up duty or any of it, Gideon. You never will. And I wouldn't want you to. I wish you'd help them, in whatever way you can."

People came and went, up and down the street, maneuvering around them. Miles frowned at her for a moment before shaking his head. "Can't do it, Vi. I have other responsibilities."

"Our first responsibility is to other people, Gideon. You know that. Especially the folks who can't help themselves. That's what you always stood for. That's why I fell in love with you. You could help them, if you wanted."

"But I—"

"And don't tell me you're too busy running the club. Why, just today you were complaining about being bored with paperwork and all the usual tediousness. I saw it in your eyes. You miss the excitement of your old life."

"Believe me, baby, I had my fill and then some of excitement."

"Don't you lie to me. I can tell."

He sighed. "The answer's no."

"Gideon, you—"

"No, Vi. That's the end of it."

Gideon Miles rarely spoke sternly to his wife, but when he did, she knew he meant it. Even then, Violet was too strong willed to roll over, but she'd at least back off for the moment.

He gave her his arm and she reluctantly took it. They continued along Decatur.

They made it only a few steps before three men blocked the sidewalk in front of them.

The men were well-dressed in expensive suits, and all three were big in the shoulders and chest. They loomed over the old couple, spread out along the sidewalk in a row, and the one in the middle smiled a nasty smile. He said, "Enjoying your nightly stroll, pops?"

Miles said nothing, sizing them up, waiting to see which way this was going to go. He gripped his cane tightly in his right hand, and with his left, he gently nudged Violet behind him.

"Asking you a question, old man," the one in the middle said in a thick Italian accent. "You having a good time with your, what you call it, nightly constitutional?"

Since he'd been in New Orleans, Miles had come to know this particular sort of hard case, possibly members of the Black Hand, preying mostly on their fellow Italian countrymen. He couldn't imagine what they wanted with him and Violet.

Miles said, "Yes. As a matter of fact, we are. Is there something I can help you with?"

The three of them crowded in, trying to intimidate him, get him to step back. Miles stood up straighter, didn't budge. He was conscious of his age right then, and of his wife behind him. This would be a fine line to walk. He knew he couldn't display any weakness to these men, but he also knew he was at a serious disadvantage.

The one in the middle did all the talking for the group. He said, "Yeah, Mr. Miles. You can help us. You can help us a lot."

He snickered, but the other two remained impassive, staring at Miles with dead, empty eyes. Miles didn't take the time to wonder how the thugs knew his name. And then the talker glanced at Violet.

"Well, well," he said. "This must be Mrs. Miles, yeah? Not a bad-lookin' old bag of bones there. Bet she was really something back in the day, huh? Bet she was a real ride, once upon a time."

Anger flared in Miles's eyes. He clenched his jaw. "You'd best watch your tongue before it gets ripped out of your mouth."

The talker cocked his head at Miles. "You know something, old man?" he said. "I truly believe that you'd try it. I truly do. But I wouldn't, if I was you. I'd hate to have to break your filthy Negro neck."

People steered clear around them, averting their eyes, hurrying past.

Miles said, "I'll ask you one more time, and I'll ask it slowly so that you understand. What … do … you … want?"

Violet gripped his hand tightly, staying half-behind him. Miles felt her moving very slightly, and knew she was reaching in her bag for the knife he'd given her years ago.

The thug on the right finally spoke, his accent so thick Miles barely understood him. "Get to the point, Antonio. We don't got all night."

The talker, Antonio, glared at his partner, then turned the glare back to Miles. "Okay, fine. Here's my point, Mr. Miles. Consider this fair warning. You stay out of Storyville, understand? You keep your nose out of whatever business transpires there. You don't do no favors for no whores, you got it?"

Miles frowned, but didn't answer.

Antonio continued, "If you go poking your nose in, it'll get cut right off your face. It's important that you understand that. Mr. Matranga takes care of the District. It's his. That's the way it is."

Miles fingers were tight on his cane.

Antonio stepped up even closer. His breath reeked of garlic. "Do you understand what I'm telling you, old man?"

The cane in Miles's hand shot up between them, jabbing Antonio hard in the chin. His mouth was half-open, and the force of the blow slammed his teeth together so hard the sound of it was like a hand clap.

He staggered back into his partners, and Miles swung the cane like a baseball bat, catching Antonio on the temple with the hard, wooden handle. Antonio dropped to the sidewalk and didn't move.

A passing woman screamed, and in a heartbeat an enormous commotion erupted all up and down the street. The two remaining thugs started toward Miles and Violet, but Violet had the knife in her hand and the thugs stopped, nervous about the look of wild intensity on the woman's face.

From up the street, someone yelled, "You there! Stop! This is the police!"

The thugs glanced at each other, and very quickly turned tail and ran off, leaving Antonio unconscious on the sidewalk.

Miles watched them light out. Once they were around the corner and out of sight, he felt the tightness leave his body, felt the rush of adrenalin subside. He turned to Violet, just as the madness was leaving her eyes and a vague fear was replacing it. He put his arm around her.

Running footsteps approached them, and they turned to face the policeman.

Except it wasn't a policeman. It was Little Cat.

The boy slowed down a few feet from them, that damnable smile spread across his face. He said, "Mr. Miles, sir. Ms. Violet. Glad to see you both well this fine evening."

Miles and Violet smiled back at him, and Violet said, "That's a fine impression of a policeman you do, Little Cat."

Cat said, "Yes, ma'am. I done heard enough of them chasing me in my time, I got the nuances of it down mighty good."

\* \* \*

Ten minutes later, they were back at the club. Miles said, "Violet, Cat. See to things. Make sure we get opened in time. I have some things I need to attend to."

Neither of them asked what he intended to do. Violet only nodded, and Cat started for the lobby to talk to the just-arriving employees.

Miles went upstairs to their set of rooms. He opened the closet, pulled out his old trunk. Inside, he found the Colt wrapped in oil cloth. He checked it thoroughly, took the time to take it apart and clean it. Then, after putting it back together, he loaded it up and held it in his hand.

It had been a few years since he'd felt the cold iron of the old Colt, and it felt good. It felt right.

He put the gun in his pocket, fished around in the trunk some more until he found the spring-loaded wrist mechanism he used for his knife. He yanked up his sleeve, strapped the thing to his forearm, and then set the blade carefully in it. He tested it two or three times, jerking his wrist just right, so that the blade slid out and into his palm.

He grinned. Just like old times.

*What would Cash Laramie think if he saw me now? Some crazy old man, about to go do something foolish.*

Hell, Cash would probably insist on joining him.

That thought gave Miles strength, and he knew it was the right thing.

He headed downstairs to tell Violet not to wait up for him.

# Four

The young whore called Celissa came barreling down the stairs in her nightgown, screeching, "Turn it off! For Christ's sake, turn it off. It's killing me!"

She stormed up to the phonograph machine, grabbed the record disc off and threw it on the floor where it smashed into pieces. The serving girl stared at her wide-eyed, and Celissa pounded her fists into her own temples, sobbing. "My head ... oh God, my head hurts so much, can't you understand? Why must you play that awful music so loudly?"

With that, she turned on her naked heel and ran back upstairs.

In the sudden silence of her departure, Gideon Miles frowned. He was sitting in the parlor of Miss Tilly's house, sipping a whiskey and soda and waiting to be seen by the Madame. The serving girl had just put the record on and wound up the machine, and all had been pleasantness and light—until the girl who hated jazz came roaring in like a five-foot-five tidal wave.

The serving girl gathered herself, turned an embarrassed smile at the visitor, said, "I do apologize, Mr. Miles. Celissa is, well ..."

"I've met Celissa already," Miles said. "No need to apologize."

The girl gathered up the bits of broken wax, saying, "Miss Tilly will be along in just a moment, sir. Is there anything I can do for you in the meantime?"

"No, that's fine."

She scurried out, and Miles was left alone in the parlor.

He sipped his drink and stared at a piece of broken record underneath the phonograph machine that the serving girl had missed. The parlor was bedecked with gold and pink wallpaper, battered tables, and lamps with frilly shades. It smelled of cigar smoke and flowery perfume.

As a marshal, oh-so-many years ago, he'd known many prostitutes. *Known* both in the Biblical sense and also in the line of his work. He'd come into contact with them on a regular basis. He knew them, understood them, even sympathized with them. And he had some suspicions about what Celissa's headaches portended.

He dwelled on that for a moment before Miss Tilly appeared in the doorway.

"I'm so pleased to see you, Mr. Miles," she said. "Have you reconsidered, sir?"

Miles stood up, bowed slightly. "I have, Miss Tilly. I'd like to speak with you."

"Of course."

She was dressed with more flamboyance than she'd been that afternoon—a rustling silk dress of red and purple, with feathers at the hip and in her hair. A very Edwardian ensemble. It occurred to Miles that brothel madams hadn't changed style in his lifetime.

The girl brought fresh drinks, and Miss Tilly perched on an over-stuffed divan. Miles settled again in the florid-print armchair.

"With your permission, Miss Tilly, I'd like to get right to the point."

"Of course. After all—"

"What interest does Charlie Matranga have in your business?"

Miss Tilly's face turned red, and she stammered, "Charlie Matranga? The gangster? I'm sure I don't—"

Miles cut her off, "Honesty in all transactions, Miss Tilly. That's how you achieve what you desire. Please, don't lie to me, madam."

Miss Tilly lowered her gaze to the carpet for a moment. When she looked at Miles again, her eyes were steely. "Please accept my apologies, Mr. Miles. You're right, of course. It's just that … the Black Hand, as I'm sure you know, is not anything to be trifled with."

"That is my understanding. But I've not had dealings with them before."

"Oh, you probably have, only you weren't aware of it. You own a nightclub, and therefore require permits and licenses and all matters of legal documentation. And if you own a business in New Orleans, you've had dealings with the Black Hand, in one form or another."

"*Hmph.*"

"How is it you've come to know my relationship to Matranga?"

"A chance meeting on the street."

"I see. Well, sir, Charlie Matranga is … he's no stranger to me. He's come to my house on numerous occasions in the last three years or so, demanding money for … protection, I suppose. He's an extortionist. And just about every house in this block pays him. If his people were actually able to protect the girls, then I would consider it money well spent. But, as you know ..."

"The girls aren't feeling particularly safe of late," Miles said.

Miss Tilly nodded. "And in the meantime, Matranga is demanding more from us."

"Is he aware of the murder of your girl Eva-Lynn? Or of any of the victims?"

"I'm sure he is. He must be. But he hasn't raised a hand, so far as I know, to find the murderer."

Miles sat back in his chair, pondering.

Miss Tilly said, "It's in the blood of a gangster, I suppose. They want power, that's all. They want to control other people's lives. In the last year or so, Charlie Matranga has been positioning himself to take over more of the District, and he's pushed hard on all the businesses here. Not just the brothels."

"When was the last time you saw Matranga?"

"It's been well over three months now. But he sends his goons around every couple of weeks. The last time I saw them here was four days ago. Again, demanding more money."

"What did you tell them?"

"I refused this time. If they can't protect us from this vicious axeman, then what good are they?"

Miles nodded thoughtfully. "Have you considered, Miss Tilly, the possibility that this murderer could be working for—"

"For Matranga? Yes, Mr. Miles, I have."

Miles shook his head, smiling. "And that's the real reason you haven't gone to the police with this, isn't it? You believe they wouldn't help you against the Black Hand."

Miss Tilly licked her lips, blinking rapidly. "Well …" she said. "They wouldn't. That's true."

"But you have no compunction against involving me in this business."

"It's not like that, Mr. Miles. This axeman—"

"Axeman, you said."

"Yes?"

"I understand that this isn't the first time an … axeman … has plagued New Orleans."

"Sadly, that's true. It wasn't long ago the so-called Axeman terrorized this city. It was before you came here, Mr. Miles, but I'm sure you've heard all about it."

"A bit. I was in Europe at the time."

"He operated in the Italian district, as I recall. Just three or four years ago."

"He was never captured. Is that correct?"

"Yes. Do you … do you think it's the same man?"

The thought seemed to alarm Miss Tilly. Miles said, "I have no idea. But it's a very real possibility, isn't it? Maybe our killer isn't working for Matranga after all."

He set his glass on the end table next to him and stood up.

"Very well," he said. "I'm still not sure what I can do to help you, Miss Tilly, but I'll look into the matter."

The madam stood as well, quickly, with her hands clasped in front of her ample bosom. "I thank you so much, Mr. Miles. I am desperate. I couldn't bear to see any of the other girls being harmed."

"In the meantime," Miles said. "I'd suggest you get your girl Celissa to a doctor."

"What? Whatever for?"

"I'm quite certain she's suffering from a venereal disease. Good night."

He left before Miss Tilly could say anything further.

# Five

On Thursday morning, Miles took a walk to the 8th District police station on Royal Street and asked the desk sergeant who was in charge of the prostitute homicides in Storyville.

The sergeant eyed him with open hostility. "Watch your tone with me, boyo. I won't have a colored man being haughty with me, I don't care how well-heeled he is."

Miles, whose tone had been conversational, cocked his head and let a cold smile play across his face. He said, "Then you're in the wrong city … boyo."

The sergeant jumped to his feet, knocking over his desk blotter as he came around the desk with fists clenched. Miles shifted his stance very slightly, ready to meet the attack. He hadn't planned on brawling with any police officers this morning, but if there was one thing sixty-plus years as a black man had taught him, it was that the need to defend oneself was ever present.

But this time there was no need. A strong voice boomed across the lobby, "Carlyle! Put a lid on it, sergeant!"

The sergeant halted, and a middle-aged man in an immaculate uniform stepped out of the shift captain's office.

"Don't you know who this is?" the captain said, stepping forward. "You're talking to Gideon Miles."

"I don't know no Gideon Miles," the sergeant said.

"Mr. Miles is a former United States Marshal, a twice-decorated war hero, and one of New Orleans most prominent citizens."

The sergeant's face turned purple with anger. "I don't care if he's Warren G. Harding. I won't have—"

"And he's quite capable of beating you to a fine pulp, sergeant. And I would feel obligated to let him. Keep. A. Civil. Tongue."

Miles smiled at the sergeant. After a moment, the copper lost his bluster and, grumbling, sat back down.

The captain turned to Miles. "How can I help you, sir?"

* * *

There was no single detective assigned to the case, much to Miles's annoyance. The police were taking great pains to keep the murders out of the spotlight, lest a connection was drawn to the old Axeman murders and another citywide panic followed.

But the captain allowed him to look through the files they had and didn't even ask why. Minor celebrity had its perks.

There wasn't much. Three dead prostitutes, all of them found in the brothels they worked in, murdered with an axe. At one scene, the murder weapon was found in a nearby alley. In another—the last, young Eva-Lynn—two witnesses had seen a big, muscular man in a wool coat leaving the scene by a window. They didn't get a good look at his face.

Sketches of all three victims had been made. Miles sorted through them. All were young and pretty, and appeared to be Creole. There was a startling sameness about their faces, a sameness that Miles recognized.

The police had zero leads, and Miles hadn't fared much better.

But he left the station with the beginnings of an idea about the killer. Just a vague one, but it was a start.

\* \* \*

He hired a cab and got off at Lee Circle. It was another humid late spring in New Orleans, and the landscaping around the Circle bloomed with fragrant lilacs and roses. Miles's starched shirt under his coat stuck to his back.

He took a moment to gaze up at the colossal monument to General Robert E. Lee, perched atop a slender Doric column, almost sixty feet high. But to Miles, whose parents had known the bondage of slavery, and had himself been born in chains, Robert E. Lee offered no inspiration.

He turned away from it and made his way to the library on St. Charles Avenue.

\* \* \*

The librarian left him in the research room with stacks of the *Times-Picayune* from 1918 and 1919, and he spent the next three hours there.

From April to August of '18, rarely did a week go by in the paper without some mention of the horrible Axeman of New Orleans. The mysterious killer struck with alarming frequency in that time, starting with an Italian grocer and his wife. Their throats were sliced open with a straight razor— the woman's so severely that her head was barely attached to her neck when they found her—and their heads bashed in with an axe. No robbery. No motive. No clues.

A little over a month later, another grocer—this one German—was attacked along with his mistress in the living quarters behind his shop. The attacker used the grocer's own hatchet to bludgeon the victims, but this time the victims survived. Their testimony was confused and contradictory, and while leading to several arrests, proved ultimately useless in finding the real attacker.

Another assault on a woman in early August had proved unsuccessful for the Axeman. But just a few days after that, he struck again.

An elderly Italian living with his two nieces was hacked with an axe as he lay in bed, the commotion drawing the attention of his nieces who ran to his aid. Both girls claimed to have seen the attacker leaving through the window, and described him as a dark, heavy man in a black coat and a slouch hat. The uncle died two days later from massive brain trauma.

The police had no solid leads, and the public howled for justice. The last murder set off a wave of hysteria in New Orleans with reported sightings of the Axeman flooding police headquarters and the entire populace gripped with a sort of frantic paranoia. A retired police detective speculated that the murderer could be the same man responsible for a string of similar murders in 1911, but no evidence of that theory ever presented itself.

As panic over the murders reached a fever pitch, the Axeman seemingly vanished.

Miles scanned the newspapers, looking for references to the killer, but as 1918 wore on, there were no new attacks, and gradually the Axeman dropped out of the headlines until March of 1919. Another Italian grocer, Charles Cortimiglia, along with his wife and two-year-old daughter, suffered a brutal attack in their beds. Cortimiglia and his wife survived, but the child was not so lucky.

The mother had been sleeping with the child in her arms when the attack came. The girl was killed instantly by an axe blow to the back of her neck. The mother suffered multiple skull fractures.

Cortimiglia himself was found in a pool of blood. A back panel on the door had been chiseled out. A bloody axe still rested on the back porch. Nothing was stolen.

Upon her recovery, Mrs. Cortimiglia accused their neighbors of the attack, despite her husband's protests. The neighbors, an elderly father and his hefty son, were arrested and tried, and the son was sentenced to death. Almost a year would go by before Mrs. Cortimiglia would retract her accusation, and the father and son set free.

And then came the letter, the infamous letter, sent to the newspapers on March 13.

It read, in part:

*Esteemed Mortal:*

*They have never caught me and they never will. They have never seen me, for I am invisible, even as the ether that surrounds your earth. I am not a human being, but a spirit and a demon from the hottest hell. I am what you Orleanians and your foolish police call the Axeman ...*

*... Undoubtedly, you Orleanians think of me as a most horrible murderer, which I am, but I could be much worse if I wanted to. If I wished, I could pay a visit to your city every night. At will I could*

*slay thousands of your best citizens, for I am in close relationship with the Angel of Death.*

*Now, to be exact, at 12:15 (earthly time) on next Tuesday night, I am going to pass over New Orleans. In my infinite mercy, I am going to make a little proposition to you people. Here it is:*

*I am very fond of jazz music, and I swear by all the devils in the nether regions that every person shall be spared in whose home a jazz band is in full swing at the time I have just mentioned. If everyone has a jazz band going, well, then, so much the better for you people. One thing is certain and that is that some of you people who do not jazz it on Tuesday night (if there be any) will get the axe ...*

*... I have been, am and will be the worst spirit that ever existed either in fact or realm of fancy.*

*The Axeman*

That night, it seemed not a single home or dance hall in New Orleans was quiet. Jazz music played from every doorway, every window, and night clubs were filled to capacity.

There were no murders that night.

A popular new tune swept the city shortly after. It was called "The Mysterious Axman's Jazz; or, Don't Scare Me Papa."

Two more attacks after that left both victims alive, but unable to offer investigators any useful information.

The final attack came on the night of October 27. The Axeman's last known victim was a man named Pepitone, head cleaved in by an axe, discovered by his wife, who was unable to tell police anything about the killer even though she saw him fleeing through an open window.

Miles placed the last newspaper on the towering stack of paper and leaned back in his chair. He rubbed the bridge of his nose and sighed wearily.

Italian grocers. How odd that so many of the victims fit that description. But not all of them. Just enough to seem unusual, without being of any use as a clue to the killer's motive.

But if the victim's ethnicity had anything to do with their murders, it made the idea of the Axeman working for Matranga and the Black Hand more feasible. After all, weren't their fellow Italians the Black Hand's primary victims?

But the victims now were prostitutes. None of them being of Italian lineage.

It struck him interesting, and disheartening, that the papers now weren't reporting on the series of axe murders in Storyville. Three dead whores and no one cared.

Miles leafed through the papers again until he found the one dated March 13, 1919. He turned to the supposed Axeman's letter, read it again.

He tossed the newspaper on the floor, unmindful of it tearing, and stood up.

If this was indeed the same killer, whether he worked for the Black Hand or not, his days were numbered. *The worst spirit that ever existed*?

*Well*, Miles thought. *We'll just have to see about that.*

# Six

Sal Ventucci was stocking the canned vegetables when the little bell over the door clanged and the three heavies came in. Matranga's boys. Again.

The one called Antonio had a black eye and a bandage on his jaw, and Sal wondered what sort of hard case could've done that to the big bastardo.

He stood up straight and wiped his trembling hands on his apron; happened every time these gangsters visited, he couldn't help it. He hated this display of fear, but his nerves betrayed him every time.

He thought of his guest, the strange young man staying in the stockroom in back, and, for some reason he couldn't quite grasp, the thought of Matranga's thugs meeting him filled Sal with dread.

"Sal," Antonio said, stepping into the store like he owned it. "We thought we'd just stop by."

It was late morning and there were no customers. Sal Ventucci and the thugs had the place to themselves. One of the goons, a mustachioed slick Sal knew as Petey, locked the door and pulled down the blind.

"Looks like you're closed," he said, in a tiny childish voice, at odds with his hulking frame.

Antonio smiled. A lower tooth was missing since the last time Sal had seen him. "We've come by, Sal, because Mr. Matranga himself is kinda shy."

"Shy? What … what do you mean?"

"Just what I say. The boss is shy. He don't like to cause a fracas, you know."

"Fracas?"

"He tries to avoid direct conflict and all. So when it looks like there could be a fracas, a little confrontation, well … he sends me and Petey and Fredrico in his stead."

The three of them started crowding in on Sal, so that the shop owner found himself forced back against the shelves. They boxed him in so close he could smell the aftershave and vague body odor from the thugs.

"See," Antonio said. "The three of us? We ain't shy."

"Now … now, listen," Sal said. "I told you. I told you boys before. I appreciate the offer, I really do. But I can't afford it, I tell you. I just don't have the money for it."

Antonio shook his head. "I think I know what the problem is here, Sal. It's a communication problem, plain and simple. See, when Mr. Matranga says 'offer,' he doesn't mean quite the same thing you and I might mean. You understand, Sal?"

"I can't give you money I don't have! For God's sake!"

"You ain't thinking it through, Sal." Antonio pushed right up against him, chest to chest. Sal's spine pressed hard against the shelves. The thug never stopped smiling. It was the smile of a simple man, and it filled Sal with terror. Brute violence was nothing to a man like that.

Someone, a potential customer, rattled the door, and Antonio put a stinking hand over Sal's face. The customer rapped on the glass. The thugs waited a long moment before the customer gave up and went away.

Antonio removed his hand and Sal breathed. He felt tears of frustration and shame rolling down his cheeks, and thought again of his guest in the stockroom, the boy his cousin had sent over to stay with him. What would happen if Antonio or Petey or Fredrico discovered him in the store? Would they beat him? Would they kill him?

Antonio said, "Where were we? Oh, yeah. I was saying, Sal, you ain't thinking it through."

A sharp, cold blade pressed into Sal's face, right below his left eye. Antonio grinned at him, so close their noses almost touched.

"There's always more money, even when you think there ain't. And you know, you can't put a price on your wellbeing. I mean, what if something … bad happened to you? What if …"

He pushed the blade harder against Sal's flesh.

"… someone came along …"

The blade edged up Sal's face, toward his eye, and blood dribbled down his jaw and plopped on his apron.

"… and just gouged out your eyeball? Eh, Sal? Then where would you be?"

The one called Fredrico spoke for the first time, a throaty, sibilant voice that made Sal want to piss himself. "Do it," he said. "Slice out his eyeball. I wanna see it."

"Should I, Sal?" Antonio said, smiling.

"Please," Sal said.

"Do it," Petey said in his little boy voice.

Antonio shrugged. "Give the people what they want," he said, and started to push the blade into the soft spot under Sal's eye.

A loud clatter came from the stockroom in back, like a bunch of pots and pans had been knocked over. All three of Matranga's men jumped, and Antonio jerked the blade away from Sal's face.

"What the hell was that?"

"Nothing," Sal said. "It's nothing."

"Someone else here, Sal, you neglect to mention?"

"It's nothing, please!"

Antonio started to say something, when the relative silence of the store was shattered by the loud scratching of a needle on wax, and the cacophonous sound of a hot jazz record blasted their eardrums.

"What the hell!" Antonio said. "Who's here, Sal?"

"A guest, only a guest!"

"Petey, go get 'em. And turn that goddamn racket off before my goddamn skull explodes!"

Petey nodded and started off for the stockroom.

Antonio turned his attention back to Sal. He had to raise his voice to be heard above the caterwauling music. "You should'a told us you had a visitor, Sal. Is it a frail? Maybe we'll have a little party."

"It's just a young man ... my cousin sent him over to stay for a few days, that's all!"

From the back, the needle scratched harshly on the record and the music came to a halt. Something thudded hard against a wall. The pots and pans clattered again, followed by another thud.

Then silence.

Antonio and Fredrico looked at each other.

Antonio called, "Petey?"

No answer.

"Petey, what's going on back there, you *cafone*?"

Still nothing. In a quieter voice, Antonio said, "Fredrico. You packing?"

Fredrico shook his head.

Antonio grimaced. He turned back to Sal. "You stay right where you are, Sal. You understand me? You move one inch and I'll gut you. Got it?"

Sal nodded, blood dripping from his face.

*  *  *

The two thugs headed for the back, Antonio leading. He held his knife in front of him, low, ready to use.

"Whoever's back there," he said. "Come out right now. If I have to come back there and get you, it won't be pretty."

There was no answer.

"You hear me, you *bastardo*? Come out now and I won't cut off your goddamn face!"

The silence from the storeroom was deafening. Matranga's men took another step toward it, and another.

Petey appeared in the doorway.

"Jesus Christ!" Antonio said.

Petey stumbled forward. Blood poured down his face from a gaping wound in his scalp. The bone of his skull gleamed in the dim electric light of the store. He staggered a step or two, looked at Antonio with dull eyes.

"Help …"

A giant loomed in the doorway behind Petey, a giant with a wide, bland face and huge arms. He held an axe in both ham fists.

He hefted the axe high, and brought it down in Petey's back. It made a meaty *chunk* sound. Petey fell into Antonio, who stumbled backward, almost losing his footing.

The giant yanked the axe out of Petey and blood spattered. With a roar that shook the walls, he swung the axe like Babe Ruth swung a bat, and cleaved Fredrico's left arm off.

Antonio was making noise, sounds that resembled words in only a vague way. As Fredrico dropped to his knees, staring at the blood that poured out of the place his arm used to be, the Axeman roared again and came for Antonio.

Blind terror had gripped Antonio's brain. He felt his trousers go wet with hot piss, and he turned and bolted for the door. Everything felt like slow-motion, like his legs were buried in molasses. He heard the giant behind him, heard pounding footsteps gaining on him.

His hand on the doorknob, he twisted it hard, hard enough to break the lock. He yanked the door open and ran, ran harder than he'd ever ran before, up the street and away from Sal Ventucci's grocery.

\* \* \*

The Axeman stood in the middle of the store, panting. Sal watched him, eyes wide with horror. Fredrico fell forward onto his face and bled out.

The Axeman turned to Sal. "I'm sorry," he said. "I'm sorry you had to see that, Mr. Ventucci."

"Oh my God."

"I really liked you, sir. I hate that it has to be this way."

"Please," Sal said.

The Axeman shook his head mournfully. "It's a hard world," he said. "Hard and unfair."

He raised the bloody weapon and brought it down in Sal Ventucci's face.

# Seven

Little Cat had said, "You oughta let me go with you, Mr. Miles, sir. A lot of them Dagoes don't like colored folk, and that's a fact. They might take a notion to beating you up. Or worse," and Gideon Miles had replied, "I'm not worried about it, Cat. You shouldn't be either. I'll be fine." Then, with a smile, "Just don't tell my wife where I'm going, okay?" And he'd left the club, taking a taxi to the Italian district.

He'd never been to that section of New Orleans before, even though geographically it wasn't far from the VioMiles. The narrow streets and winding alleys were laid out in the same way the rest of the city was, though, so he had no trouble finding his way around. He had the driver drop him at the corner of Upperline and Magnolia, said, "Pick me up here in two hours, and there'll be a substantial amount of money for you." The driver, a young Negro, nodded enthusiastically before driving off.

The grocery that once belonged to Joseph Maggio stood empty at the corner.

Miles crossed the intersection, swinging his cane, already aware of eyes on him, peering from doorways and windows. He cleared a patch of dirt off the window of the store with his cuff and peeked inside. The front of the place was stripped down to the floorboards.

He went around to the alley behind the store. It was strewn with garbage and broken bottles. The back door was locked, but the lock and knob looked flimsy. Miles glanced up and down the alley, then rammed his shoulder into the door.

The latch broke and the cheap wood splintered around it and the door opened. Miles stepped inside.

The living quarters behind the store were cramped and smelled as if a family of possums had taken up residence. There wasn't a single trace of any human having lived there.

A set of rickety stairs led up to two rooms above the store. Miles climbed the steps and stood in the larger room for a moment, then moved to the other, thinking about the nightmarish event that had occurred there three years ago. He had half-hoped the Maggio's would still be present and that he could speak to the survivors about that night. But why would they stay? He'd gained nothing by coming here, really, except maybe a sense of place. And even that had been dulled by dust and dry rot.

*Ah well*, he thought. *May as well see about questioning the neighbors, and then heading out for the residence of another victim of the Axeman.* Although he didn't foresee it going smoothly or being terribly useful.

He headed back downstairs where Antonio was standing in the open doorway leading to the alley.

The thug had a bandage on his jaw and looked less confident and intimidating than the last time Miles had seen him. Miles noted the bulge of a gun under Antonio's jacket, but with his arms at his sides the thug appeared to be making an effort to look unthreatening.

Miles stopped halfway down the steps. "If you're aiming to get a little grocery shopping done, you're about three years too late."

Antonio knitted his brow. "Grocery? .... Oh, right. No, it's nothing like that."

"What do you want?"

Antonio showed his hands. "Nothing bad. I ain't here for trouble. We been following you is all, and Mr. Matranga sent me in to fetch you."

Miles bristled. "*Fetch* me? Nobody fetches me, boy."

"Oh, for ... don't be so touchy. Mr. Matranga has requested the pleasure of your company. How's that?"

Miles frowned. "Where are your partners?"

"Well ... that's the thing. That's part'a what he wants to talk to you about."

"Part?"

"Look," Antonio said. "The boss is waiting in the auto, just outside. And he wants to talk to you. I swear we ain't got anything shifty planned. He just wants to have a few words."

Miles crossed his arms. "You insulted my wife. By all rights, I should knock your teeth out."

"You already knocked out one of them." Antonio pulled his lower lip down, showed Miles the space where the tooth had been. "And I'm sorry, okay? What do I have to say? The thing is, we got bigger problems."

"What sort of problems?"

"Well, Mr. Miles, that's what Mr. Matranga wants to see you about. Will you pretty goddamn please come out and talk to him?"

Miles grinned in spite of himself and descended the rest of the stairs. "Lead on, Antonio. But if you get dodgy, I won't hesitate to plant this cane upside your head."

"Duly noted, old man."

Antonio led Miles outside and around to Magnolia Street. A long, shiny touring car with a closed canopy waited there, motor running. The front was open, and the Negro driver behind the wheel didn't turn his head or acknowledge Miles or Antonio.

Antonio opened the rear door and held it for Miles. Miles was keenly aware that this could be a setup, and he took a second to weigh it. But if they wanted to kill him, they could have done it easily and without fuss in Maggio's grocery store with a single well-placed bullet.

He got in the auto, and Antonio slid in after him.

Two cushioned benches faced each other in the riding compartment; Matranga had the one facing them all to himself. He was an unremarkable-looking man, moderately overweight, with curly black hair that no amount of pomade could quite keep under control. His suit was tailored, but a bit garish for Miles's taste. He said, "Gideon Miles. You're a bit famous, aren't you?"

"Not terribly," Miles said. "Buffalo Bill never asked me to be in his Wild West show."

Matranga tapped the roof with the top of an elegantly-carved cane, and the auto started moving. "Of course not," he said. "You're much too understated for that sort of thing, aren't you? No limelight or center stage for the great, colored U.S. Marshal. The somber, stoic hero of the—"

"Matranga," Miles said. "Let's skip the dime novel poetry. I'm a busy man."

Matranga laughed without humor. "So it seems. You've been looking into these dead whores, yes? Been looking for the phantom Axeman."

"And just how would you know about my business?"

"Nothing happens in Storyville without me knowing about it."

"I've heard that about you."

Matranga nodded. He reached into his inner jacket pocket for a cigar, stuck it in his mouth. Antonio leaned forward with a lit match, and Matranga puffed fragrant smoke until it was burning to his satisfaction.

Puffing, he said, "I knew all about you, Gideon—may I call you Gideon?—before you'd even filled out all the paperwork on that nightclub of yours. And you need to remind yourself that you wouldn't be in business if not for my good graces. Especially considering I'm not overly fond of coloreds."

Miles leaned forward in his seat. "That's fine," he said. "Because I'm not partial to low-life gangsters. And it's *Mr.* Miles."

He felt Antonio stiffen next to him, but kept his eyes locked on Matranga's. The boss's face darkened for a long moment and the atmosphere in the auto went stormy with impending violence.

Then Matranga sighed and said, "I'll give you this, *Mr.* Miles. You've got guts. I truly do admire that."

"I don't give a damn about your admiration, Matranga. And if this conversation isn't going anywhere, you can let me off at the corner."

They were all silent for several seconds. Miles and Matranga stared each other down, and Antonio fidgeted in his seat.

Finally, Matranga said, "Just to be clear, if there's any doubt, this so-called Axeman is *not* in my employ. As a matter of fact, he is now my number one enemy."

"Why is that? You suddenly interested in the well-being of Storyville's prostitutes?"

"Pah. Hardly. I came here from New York four years ago to make money, not wet-nurse a bunch of feral bitches. My concern is with my own men. You see, we had an up-close and personal encounter with the Axeman yesterday. And now two of my most trusted employees are dead. Antonio here barely escaped with his life."

Miles looked at Antonio, whose eyes were haunted and scared at the memory of what had happened. Miles had supposed Antonio's less aggressive manner had something to do with their previous encounter. He saw now that he'd given himself too much credit. "What happened?"

"Antonio, tell him."

Antonio cleared his throat. In a quiet voice, he said, "Me and Fredrico and Petey dropped in on … on a friend of ours, fella who runs a grocery on Upperline. The Axeman was there. He chopped them … to pieces. With a goddamn axe."

Matranga said, "Last night's paper says the guy who ran the grocery got killed, too. Surprised you haven't heard about it."

Miles said, "I haven't seen a paper since yesterday morning." Miles leaned back and processed the information. "So what, exactly, do you want from me, then?"

Antonio said, "This grocer—Sal Ventucci—he told us that the killer knew his … his cousin. And that this cousin had sent him to stay in his back room for a while."

"And," Matranga said. "With two of my men in the morgue, the buttons are looking at me very closely right now. I can't really make a move to look into things myself."

"Again," Miles said, "what do you want from me?"

This time it was Matranga's turn to lean forward. He took the cigar out of his mouth and said, "Mr. Miles, I have a proposition for you."

# Eight

They let him out in front of the VioMiles. He watched them drive off, thought about the poor cab driver he'd asked to come back for him, and wondered how long he would wait for his fare before giving up. But the driver only occupied his thoughts for a moment. He had much more pressing things to consider now.

Angrier than a hornet, Violet was on him the moment he stepped in the foyer. "Gideon Miles, you old fool, I've half a mind to slap you silly!"

"Now, Vi—"

"Don't you 'now, Vi' me. Going off all by yourself to some neighborhood where they're likely to do horrible things to any old black man they see. What were you thinking?"

Little Cat stood behind her, looking chagrined. "I'm sorry, Mr. Miles, she made me tell."

"Made you tell!" Violet said. "You two keeping secrets from me now?"

Miles said, "Vi, you're the one wanted me to look into this in the first place."

"Look into it, yes, but I don't want you risking your fool neck for it!"

"Risking my neck? Christ, Vi, what did you expect? I'm looking for a man who chops people with an axe!"

Flustered, she came back at him. "Forget all about it, then. I changed my mind. I don't want you to look into anything. I want you safe and sound, here with me."

Most of the anger had left her voice already, replaced by genuine anxiety. Miles touched her cheek. "Vi, baby, you don't have anything to worry about."

"But I do worry."

He sighed. "I was a U.S. Marshal, Vi. I know my strengths and I know my limitations."

"I'm not so sure you know your limitations."

Little Cat said, "Maybe I should go ... um, check on something?"

Vi turned on him, anger flaring again. "Like what, Little Cat? What should you check on, exactly?"

"Oh, anything, ma'am. Anything at all."

"You're not going anywhere yet, you vagabond. You're in this just as deep as my husband."

"Yes, ma'am."

"Now, Vi—"

"What did I say about that 'now, Vi' business?"

"Okay," Miles said, raising his hands. "I should've told you where I was going. I won't keep anything else from you, and I'm sorry I did this time. That wasn't fair of me. But, Vi, there won't be any dropping the matter now."

"Gideon—"

"I intend to see this through, Vi, and you're going to have to trust that I know what I'm doing."

Violet looked as if she wanted to say something else, but couldn't find the right words. Finally, she shook her head and laughed weakly. "I know you do, Gideon," she said.

"You always have." Then, "Good Lord, why did I have to go and marry a lawman? What was I thinking?"

Miles grinned. "You *weren't* thinking. I had your head spinning too much for thinking."

She grinned back. "You sure did. Why, the way you—"

Little Cat said, "I really do need to go check on something—anything—before ya'll continue."

Miles and Violet laughed, and Violet said, "We'll save the sweet talk for another time. And don't you think this argument is over. It's just on hold."

"Fair enough."

"So tell me, fearless husband, what did you learn on your foray into the dreaded Italian district?"

\* \* \*

Matranga's organization had eyes and ears everywhere. It hadn't been hard for them to find Sal Ventucci's cousin—a carpenter named Giano Carletti, who lived on La Harpe. Miles noted that the address wasn't far from the home of the Besumer's, the Axeman's second set of victims.

"You track this *bastardo* down for me," Matranga had said. "You find him and not involve the buttons, and I'll leave the whores in Storyville to their own devices."

"How do I know you'll do what you say?" Miles had asked, and Matranga had replied, "You don't know me very well, so I'll let that slide. But I'm a man of my word. Not like these young swells coming up now with no integrity. If I say it, it's a bond. Besides, Storyville's more trouble than it's worth these days."

Miles had believed him, saying, "That's a deal, Matranga," and the two men had shook hands on it.

And now Miles stood in front of Giano Carletti's home, gripping his cane, feeling the weight of the Colt in his coat pocket. Little Cat was with him, on Violet's insistence.

"Wait on the corner, Cat," Miles said.

"But Ms. Violet said to—"

"Wait on the corner."

Little Cat shrugged. "She's gonna kill you. And then she's gonna kill me into the bargain."

"Everything will be fine. Just stay alert. I won't be long."

Little Cat grumbled but did as he was told, shoving his hands in his pockets and ambling down to the corner. Miles approached the house. It was a crackerbox on a modest street, made with cheap materials but well-tended. There was a scraggly tree in the yard and a swinging bench on the small porch.

A woman appeared at the screen door before Miles had even set foot on the porch. She peered at him, her features hidden behind the screen, and said in a heavy Italian accent, "Yes? What do you want?"

Miles took off his hat. "Forgive me for bothering you, ma'am. I'm looking for Mr. Carletti."

"For what?"

"I need to speak to him about his cousin, Sal."

"You don't know his cousin. His cousin wasn't friends with any Negroes."

"I didn't say we were friends, ma'am. I take it you've heard about what happened to him?"

"God rest his soul." The woman moved behind the screen, and Miles got a glimpse of dull gray hair and a hard, distrustful face. "What do you have to do with my husband's cousin?"

"Nothing, directly. I'm looking into his death."

"You a policeman? There are no colored policemans."

Miles thought about correcting her, but decided it wasn't important. He said, "I have some information, Mrs. Carletti, that I think your husband should know." He didn't mention that Mr. Carletti already knew. That tidbit wouldn't get him in the door.

"Mr. Carletti is busy. You go away. Leave us—"

A masculine voice from behind her said, "It's fine, Rosa. I'll speak to him."

"But, Giano—"

"Let him in, dear."

Mrs. Carletti reluctantly unlatched the screen door and held it open. Miles said, "Thank you, ma'am," and stepped inside.

\* \* \*

Where Mrs. Carletti was hard and angular, her husband was smooth-faced as a baby with dull, cow eyes. He ushered Miles into a small sitting room, overcrowded with hand-crafted furniture and photographs and paintings on every available inch of wall space. Mrs. Carletti huffed and stormed off to the kitchen without a word. Carletti motioned Miles to the sofa, sat himself in a polished oak arm chair.

"Jimmy killed Sal, didn't he?" Carletti said in a willowy, weak voice with no trace of an accent. "It was Jimmy. And I sent him there. God have mercy on me, but it's my fault Sal is dead."

"Jimmy?" Miles said.

I should've known. I should have realized. He was never right in the head. Back in '17, I … I suspected. And when Jimmy left for New York, I knew. I just knew."

Miles said, "Mr. Carletti. Who is Jimmy?"

Carletti looked at the floor. "Jimmy Manta. He used to work for me at my shop. My apprentice. He had the makings of a fine carpenter, he really did. But I always knew. I mean, I always had an inkling, I guess you could say, that there was something … wrong with him."

Tears pooled in the man's eyes, and Miles thought, not without some pity, that Carletti was a very weak man. It wasn't in the tears so much as the posture, the unwillingness to look Miles in the face. Miles had met men like him before. Wyoming was studded with their graves.

But it was a new time now, a new place, where weak men weren't destroyed immediately—they were destroyed inch by inch, murdered slowly by stronger men in an indifferent world. It was a much crueler time now, Miles thought.

He said, "Jimmy Manta worked for you in 1917?"

Carletti nodded. "He worked for me until the end of that year. He started three years before that, when he was only a boy. Fifteen years old. He was an orphan. I mean, that's … that's what he told me. I assume it's true, but who can say?"

"And he left for New York that year?"

"Yes. Was trying to find his father, he said. And I have to admit, I was relieved. Toward the end, he had become quick tempered. He would get so mad, you know? About nothing. Some grocer over-charged him once and he couldn't talk of anything but getting revenge for the slight. I think … well, I think that's why all those grocery store owners were killed."

"You think Jimmy did it? You think he was the Axeman?"

"Oh God. I just don't know. But he would get so agitated and angry, and he talked all the time about his father, how he hated the man for abandoning him, and music. Jazz, jazz, jazz, all the time. He was obsessed with it."

The sitting room was close and hot. Miles ran a finger under his collar. "Mr. Carletti. When did Jimmy come back?"

Carletti still wouldn't meet his gaze. "Eight months ago. Eight months and two weeks. I remember because he came to my door the day after my wife left for Italy. She went to visit her family for the winter, and only came home two weeks ago. That's why Jimmy had to leave. My wife wouldn't have stood for him staying here. And he'd gotten worse. I mean, mentally. I think he had the … well …"

"You think he had the what?"

Carletti glanced at the doorway, as if to make sure his wife wasn't eavesdropping. "I think he had the syphilis," he whispered.

Miles frowned. "Why do you think that?"

"I knew men who'd had it. I know the signs. My uncle had it. So when Rosa came home, I told him he couldn't stay anymore, Rosa wouldn't like it. So he took his knapsack and his phonograph and records and left."

"Two weeks ago? Is that when he went to stay in your cousin's stockroom?"

The tears in Carletti's eyes spilled over. He held his head in his hands. "Oh, Sal, what have I done? *Mi dispiace tanto, mai cugino, mai la famiglia* ..."

Miles gave him a moment to collect himself, then said, "Did he ever find his father in New York?"

"He ... he never said. I don't think so."

"Did he work for you again when he came back?"

It took Carletti a minute to answer, but he finally wiped the tears away and sniffed, "Just for room and board. Business has been bad. I couldn't afford to pay him wages. But when I sent him to Sal, I told him that Sal could pay him a little for helping out in the grocery. Sal, God keep him, was thankful for the help. And I didn't ... I didn't say a word to Sal about my misgivings."

Carletti burst into tears, sobbing into his hands.

His wife appeared in the doorway, face like stone and arms crossed over her small breasts.

"You leave now," she said. "Leave my husband alone. Go away."

Miles nodded. He put on his hat and saw himself out.

# Nine

Jimmy Manta had been wandering. He'd left Ventucci's grocery by the back door, leaving the axe behind but taking the time to shove his record collection in a burlap sack. He had to leave the phonograph machine. It pained him to do so, but he could always get another.

He'd made his way down to the Garden District, walked for several hours along St. Charles Avenue and Magazine Street. He thought about nothing for a long time before making his way to Audubon Park. He found a dark spot under a giant oak near a lagoon, stretched out there, and fell asleep.

Amazingly, the coppers didn't roust him, and he woke up with the gray dawn edging in. He knew, finally, where he was going. Back to LaHarpe. Back to Mr. Carletti. He would help him. He had to.

He trudged along, the burlap sack slung over his shoulder. His stomach rumbled, but he drowned it out by humming to himself, "There'll Be Some Changes Made" and "Heebie Jeebies" and "Bleeding Hearted Blues."

It was late morning when he made it to Carletti's street.

And stopped.

There was a young Negro standing on the corner opposite, hands in pockets, looking bored and a little surly. The Negro captured his attention because there weren't any on this block, which was mostly German and Italian. But also because Manta had an undeniable fascination with colored boys of that particular type. It was nothing sexual—he was no pervert—but more a vague sense of envy. The jazz Manta loved so dearly came from *this* type. This charmingly insolent sort of Negro.

But he couldn't possibly have any business here, no *good* sort of business anyway.

The killer crossed the street north at the intersection, away from the boy. He walked up half a block, and then positioned himself behind one of the oak trees that lined the street. He peered around the trunk. Just in time to see the front door of the Carletti home swing open and another black man come out.

This one was much older, maybe in his sixties, but still fit and powerful-looking. He wore a good suit, if not a little muted and modest. Right away, there was something about him that made the killer anxious.

The old man walked with the speed and assurance of someone half his age, swinging a hickory cane, up the street to the younger Negro waiting there. The young man came to attention and the two of them conferred for a moment. Then they started southeast, toward St. Bernard Avenue.

The killer followed at a distance, sweating. His heart pounded double time with fear. The old man. He was bad news. The killer knew it in his gut.

They stopped at St. Bernard and hailed a passing taxi cab. The killer hurried as the taxi drove off, and was lucky enough to snag another one. He only had a few coins in his pocket, could scarcely afford a taxi, but it was vitally important to know where the old man was going, where he was from, what he wanted.

He told the driver to follow, and the next few minutes were spent in mounting terror as they took left and right and left again, and the killer imagined all sorts of disastrous scenarios.

The first taxi turned onto Rue St. Louis, and at the intersection with Royal Street let the old man and the young swell off in front of a club called the VioMiles.

The killer knew the place. He'd been there once before, right after he'd come back to New Orleans. It was a fairly new place for well-heeled types who didn't have to worry about coppers not letting them booze it up. And they always had live bands playing hot jazz.

And it all came clear to him as he got out of his taxi at the opposite corner. He knew who the old man was. The *Times-Picayune* had done a sensational piece on him not long ago.

The owner of the VioMiles.

The semi-famous Negro U.S. Marshal.

Gideon Miles.

The killer's heart fluttered but he breathed deeply and concentrated on calming himself. *"The stars that shine above,"* he sang under his breath. *"Will light our way to love ... ah you rule this world with me, I'm the Sheik of Araby ..."*

He had the advantage here. He knew who his enemy was. Not the coppers, not the Black Hand, not anyone but Gideon goddamn Miles.

# Ten

By 12:30, the VioMiles was hopping. In a remarkably short period of time, the club had become one of the premier destinations in the Quarter, attracting top talent to the stage, and by proxy club-goers with taste and money to burn. Gideon Miles had never intended the club to be for the elite types, black or white, but he wasn't complaining.

Kid Ory's Band was playing for the fourth weekend in a row, back temporarily from a spell in Los Angeles, and featuring a young trumpet player called Armstrong. The dance floor was packed with couples dancing in ways that boggled Miles's mind. Thirty years earlier, he'd seen people arrested for less provocative things.

Cigar smoke hung thick in the air, along with the tang of fine booze, raucous laughter, popping champagne corks. All to the syncopated beat of Kid Ory's laconic drummer.

Violet was in the kitchen, overseeing the wait staff. Little Cat's duties as concierge kept him jumping between the packed foyer, the dining area and the hall. And Miles watched it all from the second floor balcony, hidden from most angles by heavy red drapes.

He smoked his pipe and thought about this strange new world he'd somehow managed to survive into. Hell, not only survive, but thrive. He was well off now, very nearly wealthy, even. He remembered days on the trail, living rough, thinking one day he'd leave it all behind and enjoy the Good Life.

And here the Good Life was, right in front of him. Everything he and Vi had worked for, everything they'd dreamed of.

So why wasn't he enjoying it?

He had to admit it—the last couple of days, on the trail again, tracking down a vicious murderer, he felt more alive and focused than he'd felt in a very long time.

Trouble was just in his blood.

Imagining what Violet would say if he told her any of that made him smile. Best keep that one under his hat, he thought.

Near the bar, Little Cat was waving, trying to get his attention. The young man gestured toward the other end of the bar. Miles scanned the patrons there, spotted a prominent city councilman with a sizeable group of hangers-on.

Miles sighed. The councilman would want to bend his ear a bit, flaunt his connection to the famous lawman-turned-club owner, and Miles would have to smile and endure his company, at least for a few minutes.

He headed downstairs.

\* \* \*

Jimmy Manta waited in the alley behind the VioMiles.

Two busboys came out to smoke. One of them was fat, wearing a white frock that would fit him well enough. But he held back, watching from the shadows behind a cluster of garbage cans. He didn't want to risk two at once.

A little later, a few members of Kid Ory's band came out and shared a marijuana cigarette. Manta watched them, fascinated. He could smell the sharp, earthy scent of their smoke, and tried to hold his breath. Reefer scared him a bit.

Another hour passed, the fat busboy came out again, alone this time. He lit his smoke and leaned against the brick wall.

The Axeman approached him quickly and without a sound. The busboy never saw him. With one sharp movement, Manta snapped the fat busboy's neck.

He put on the busboy's frock, steeled his nerves, and went inside.

\* \* \*

Miles managed to break free of the councilman and his syncophantic cronies. He made a slow circuit of the club, easing past clusters of laughing, boisterous patrons and furiously dancing couples. He shook the occasional hand, smiled, played the part.

Near the kitchen entrance, a large busboy hustled past him, jarring his shoulder.

"Pardon me, sir, sorry," the busboy said, hurrying on into the crowded hall. Miles didn't get a good look at him. It wouldn't have mattered anyway—Violet did all the hiring for the kitchen staff, and Miles wouldn't have recognized most of them.

In the kitchen, he mentioned the rude busboy to his wife, but she was far too busy to do anything other than offer him a quick peck on the cheek.

"Let's give up the club," Miles said. "Let's move back to Wyoming."

"Get out of my kitchen, husband."

He shrugged and went back out to the hall. Kid Ory's band was doing a rambunctious version of "Tiger Rag" and the new, young horn player, Armstrong, was playing an amazingly inventive solo. Miles stood and watched as the patrons went crazy.

\* \* \*

No one paid any attention to the killer when he ducked behind the stage. The one time he'd been at the club before, he'd seen Gideon Miles go that way, and then appear moments later at the balcony. The stairs were easy to spot. He headed up them.

The door at the top was locked. The killer twisted the knob, put his shoulder into it, but the door wouldn't budge. Sweat poured down his brow, and he felt several long seconds of anxiety.

Kid Ory's band blistered through "Tiger Rag," a song the killer knew very well. In another few seconds, the horn solo would end and the rest of the band would come tearing in. The song would be at its loudest and wildest.

He waited for it, and when the other instruments thundered to life, he kicked the door in. He could scarcely hear the crash of wood himself, standing right next to it.

The space where the Miles's lived was roomy and a little Spartan. There were pictures on the walls of horses and Western scenes. A solid oak Grandfather clock. Simple furniture. Lots of books. Manta noted with some disdain that there was no phonograph or even a radio. What the hell did these people do with their time? Read books, for God's sake?

He pulled a letter he'd written out of his pocket. It was already crumpled and limp with sweat. He put it on an end table, then worried that it would be overlooked somehow, so picked it up and put it on another end table.

He started to leave.

The noise from the club came in through the open balcony doors, and the killer couldn't resist. The band was too good, the new trumpet soloist was too amazing. He wanted to see. He wanted to see the tops of heads and the dancing whores and the gleaming sweat on the horn player's face.

He moved the heavy drapes aside, very slightly, and peeked through.

* * *

Miles happened to glance up at his balcony and saw the heavy red drapes flutter. He saw a shadow play across them and disappear.

He frowned. Aside from Violet and himself, Little Cat was the only one authorized to be upstairs in the living quarters. Miles knew Violet was still in the kitchen. Was Little Cat up there for some reason? He glanced around and spotted his young protégé near the bandstand, chatting up an attractive young woman.

Miles cursed himself for leaving the Colt up there, and hurried to the narrow staircase behind the stage.

When he reached the foot of the stairs, Manta came through the kicked-in door at the top. Their eyes locked and neither of them moved for a second that stretched out long. The noise of the band was deafening.

The Axeman roared and barreled down the steps.

Miles moved to meet him.

Halfway up, Miles dropped face-down on the steps, and Manta's shoe hit him in the shoulder. Manta lost his footing, grabbed uselessly for the handrail, then tumbled down the stairs.

Miles was on his feet in half a second, ignoring the pain in his shoulder. Manta lay at the bottom of the steps, eyes wide open with the breath knocked out of him. Miles hurried after him.

In the seconds it took Miles to reach him, Manta had recovered. He was pulling himself up by the bannister. From three steps above, Miles kicked him in the face.

Manta grunted, stumbled back. Miles pressed the small advantage, swinging a wide left at the killer's stunned face. The blow connected against the killer's nose, and Miles felt the satisfying snap of cartilage.

In Miles's experience, most men who'd taken a fist to the nose that hard would be down for the count. So he was surprised when Manta shook it off and threw a sloppy punch of his own. Miles sidestepped it but couldn't avoid the big man's bulk when he moved to tackle him.

They went stumbling back against the bannister, hard enough to snap it off, and Miles felt jagged wood dig into his spine. The killer had him around the torso, and Miles rained blows down on the big, round head.

Manta snapped his head up hard into Miles's chin. Stars glittered in Miles's vision. Then the killer had both huge hands around his throat, throttling.

Miles didn't attempt to pry the massive fingers from his throat. That would have been useless. Instead, he did something only slightly less useless, punching the madman in the face over and over, with both fists.

But Manta's grip didn't loosen, despite the cuts and bruises and blood all over his face. If anything it got tighter, and the stars in Miles's vision were starting to go dim.

Something moved behind Manta. Miles heard a faint *thud*, and the fingers around his throat loosened. He fell back into the stairs, saw Manta spinning around to face the new threat. It was Little Cat. He had something big and solid in his hands, swung it hard, and hit Manta in the face. The killer cried out in frustration and pain, clutching his face. He shoved past Cat and made for the hall.

"Stop him!" Miles croaked from the bottom of the steps.

Little Cat looked at him. "Stop him?" he said. "Mr. Miles, sir, did you see the size of that man?"

Despite everything that had just happened, the expression on Cat's face almost made Miles chuckle. He saw that the kid was holding one of the big, silver standing ashtrays that decorated the club. The heavy end of it was dented and smeared with blood.

Cat set the ashtray down and offered a hand to help Miles up. Miles braced himself for a moment against the part of the bannister that wasn't broken and struggled to get his breath back. His adrenaline was still pumping, but he suspected his old bones would register the pain soon enough.

"Cat," he said. "That makes the second time you've saved my ancient carcass."

Cat grinned. "I'm mighty useful to have around, I reckon."

"That you are."

"Was that … was that who I think it was?"

Miles nodded. "I expect so." He glanced up at the kicked-in door to his living quarters. "Looks like Jimmy Manta the Axeman decided to drop in for a visit."

# Eleven

*Dearest Mr. Gideon Miles,*

*You can imagine my delight upon learning that you have deemed to pursue me. I consider it an honor. All of the Souls that burn with me in the deepest Regions of Hell now burn brighter with envy at my new station. You will, of course, fail. Not even a man of your considerable skills can lay hands on a Dark Spirit. But that is beside the point. You will try, won't you, and that alone pleases me.*

*You think me a monster, and you are right. But as you know, I love jazz. You might call it my weakness, but it is, in fact, a source of strength. I am a sporting type and so propose this to you:*

*On Saturday night, I intend to roam your earthly realm again. I will claim another prize. As is my wont, I will pass over the houses that are swinging it.*

*But there will be one with no music in her. She will be chosen to get the axe.*

*I await with much anticipation to witnessing your attempts to stop me.*

*Yours, from the Pit.*

\* \* \*

The letter felt greasy in Miles's fingers. He set it down on the end table where he'd found it and wiped his fingers on his trousers.

Violet sat on the sofa opposite him, hands crossed on her lap. Tears brimmed in her eyes and her lower lip trembled. She said, "He knows who you are."

"Yes."

"How?"

"I don't know. But it doesn't matter. I know who he is as well. And I know who he intends to go after."

"Fine," Violet said. "Then call the police. Tell them. Let them stop him."

Miles shook his head. "I made a deal with Matranga to leave the police out of it."

Violet said, with some bitterness, "You're making deals with gangsters now? There was a time, Gideon, when you never would have done something like that."

Miles clenched his jaw. "The world has changed, Violet. I play it the way I promised, and Matranga stays out of Storyville."

"Then call your gangster friends and let them deal with it!"

Miles stood up, his anger flaring. "Damnit, Violet, you're not being reasonable!"

Violet stood up as well to face him, her nose inches from his. "No, Gideon, *you're* not being reasonable. This man almost killed you! I know you're a strong and capable man, but you're 67 years old! You can't get around that. In your heart you're as strong as ever, but … you're human, Gideon. You're the best man I've ever known, but you're a man. Just a man. And you don't have the sense to be scared."

Tears rolled down her face, and Miles felt a deep stab of guilt for causing her pain. She deserved better.

In a softer voice, he said, "Vi, baby ... you're wrong. I am scared. If I wasn't before, I am now. I promise you, I have no interest in dying just yet, and earlier tonight ... I thought for sure I was a goner. Yes, it scared me. It terrified me, but mostly because I never felt that ... helpless before."

"Gideon—"

"And that's why I have to finish this. I wish there was some way I could make you understand."

He gave her his handkerchief and she dabbed at her eyes. "I do understand, Gideon. I always have. But, you know, that never made it any easier."

He took her chin in his hand, looked her in the eyes, and thought that, after all these long, long years, she was still the most beautiful girl he'd ever seen.

"I'm sorry, Vi."

She said, "This isn't the Wild West, Gideon. And you don't have anything to prove anymore."

"I know that. I'm not trying to prove anything."

"Yes, you are. You're trying to prove something to yourself."

He started to deny the accusation, but stopped. It was uncomfortably close to the truth.

"Listen," he said. "I'll have Little Cat with me. And I'll be armed. I may not be as agile as I used to be, but I'm still damn good with a revolver."

She cocked an eyebrow at him. "When, exactly, was the last time you fired that Colt?"

He cleared his throat. "Not that long ago."

"I think it's been years."

"No, he said. "Not that long."

"Did you even shoot a gun when we were in France?"

He said, "Woman, you really are a big, old pain in my neck."

She smiled feebly. "Until the day we both die, husband."

He took her in his arms and held her for a long time.

# Twelve

Violet stayed close to him all day Saturday. They went out for a walk after lunch, but otherwise stayed in their living quarters, reading and talking. They didn't discuss what Miles would do that evening.

Mid-morning, he placed a telephone call to New York, and by early afternoon the operator rang back with the call. He talked with the party for a few minutes, asking some very specific questions, then rang off.

When it started getting dark, Miles put on a good suit, strapped on his old holster, slid the Colt into it. He put on a light overcoat that hid the rig from casual sight. Violet didn't cry or get angry. She kissed him and said, "Be safe."

Miles and Little Cat hired an auto and drove down to the District.

\* \* \*

The clientele at Miss Tilly's place was exclusively white and didn't respond well to seeing two Negroes walk in. Miles found that the older he got, the more perverse pleasure he took from upsetting bigots. He wasn't proud of that, but he wasn't particularly ashamed, either.

Miss Tilly greeted them hurriedly, looking nervous. "Mr. Miles, Mr. Borre … what on Earth brings you here this time of night?"

Miles said, "Is Celissa working?"

"Well, no," Miss Tilly said. "After all, you advised …
that is to say …" Her wide face ran through a variety of
shades of red. She looked over her shoulder at the clients
lounging in the parlor, drinking whiskey, playing billiards,
chatting up the scantily-clad whores. More than a few of
them were distracted now, glaring at the colored interlopers
on their debauchery.

"Is she in her room?"

"Yes. But, as I say, she's not working until … I mean
…" She lowered her voice to an embarrassed whisper. "The
doctor said it would take a couple of days until he knows
if—"

"That's fine," Miles said. "Take us up there."

"But—"

Little Cat said, "Don't argue with the man, lady."

It was uncharacteristically rough for Cat, and Miss Tilly
and Miles both looked at him. "*What?*" Cat said. "It's what
you call an urgent situation, right?"

Miss Tilly laughed a shrill, false laugh and said, very
loudly, "The problem is right upstairs, gentlemen, thank you
for coming by so quickly," and proceeded to lead them to
the second floor.

The upstairs was less ornate than downstairs, just a dim
floor lamp placed at the long hall's halfway point. All the
doors were closed. Behind some of them, jazz played, or
waltzes, or old European ballads. And behind almost all of
them, bedsprings creaked and men grunted and bottles
clinked against glasses.

Miles found it all horribly depressing.

He took Miss Tilly by her upper arm and spoke in a low, urgent tone as they walked. "You need to listen to me very closely, and keep your head. Our Axeman intends to strike tonight. Here. And his target is Celissa."

"Celissa? But, why—"

"Why is of no import right now. What matters is that you follow my instructions without fail. When he shows tonight, he'll ask for her, and you'll take him to her."

Miss Tilly tried to stop walking, but Miles dragged her along. She stuttered, "My Lord, Mr. Miles, I can't just—"

"You can and you will. Little Cat and I will be waiting for him. This ends tonight."

"But what—"

"You'll bring him right to Celissa's room, and then you'll telephone Matranga and tell him to come right away. You do know how to contact him, yes?"

Miss Tilly nodded dumbly. She said, "This ... this is madness."

Cat said, "Ma'am, you don't know the half of it. This fella is big."

Miles patted the Colt in its holster. "Nothing to worry about," he said. "I have an equalizer."

He only wished he felt as confident as he sounded.

* * *

Celissa was not pleased at being disturbed from her sleep. She lifted her head from the pillow, scowling, and snapped, "Why are you here? You promised I'd be left alone! Go away!"

Miss Tilly said, "Celissa, we—"

"Don't talk! Please, don't speak, I can't stand the noise, it's killing me!"

She broke off into sobs, burying her face in the pillow.

Miles said, "Miss Tilly. Get her to another room."

Miss Tilly tried to ease the girl up. "Don't touch me!" Celissa wailed into the pillow, swatting blindly at the madam.

Miles frowned. "Fine," he said. "Little Cat and I will do it."

The girl started screaming, clutching her skull and rolling back and forth on the bed. Cat said, "Oh, Lordy. I haven't had to wrassle a screaming woman in … well, days."

It took ten minutes for the three of them to get Celissa to Miss Tilly's room. Celissa kicked and screamed and wailed the whole way, and Miles realized the girl was much farther gone than he would have guessed. Her condition had deteriorated dramatically in only a few days. Even with treatment, he suspected Celissa wasn't long for this world.

They dumped her on Miss Tilly's bed, where she went limp and sobbed pitiably. Cat wiped his brow and Miss Tilly wrung her hands, "She's gotten worse, just since this afternoon," she said. "Oh, the poor thing."

Coldly, Miles said, "It's a shame you weren't more diligent. And who knows how many she's infected?"

"I'll have you know—"

"Save it. You see yourself as the protector of these girls, don't you? Well, I reckon you've done a poor job of it."

Miss Tilly looked at Miles, and then Celissa, before casting her gaze to the floor. There were tears in her eyes.

"If I'd known," she said.

"If you'd known, you'd have taken her off the line and replaced her with someone else, right? That's how commerce works, doesn't it? But you didn't. I'll tell you something, Miss Tilly. From a certain perspective, you're the one responsible for the Axeman."

She shook her head. "I don't see how that's possible."

"You don't yet, but you will. Now head back downstairs. Cat and I will be in Celissa's room. Do I need to instruct you again on what to do?"

Miss Tilly wiped her eyes and shook her head.

"Good. Now go."

\* \* \*

Miles sat in the ragged armchair and Cat paced back and forth, twirling Miles's cane. Miles watched him, admiring the kid's energy but also worried that he was too high-strung for the job ahead.

"Cat," he said. "Calm yourself. Sit down."

"Sit down? I'm sorry, Mr. Miles, but I don't think I can do that. I have a little nervous energy on account of us being about to face a crazy, axe-wielding killer and all."

"We'll be fine."

"That's easy for you to say, sir. Not all of us are big, bad U.S. Marshals from the wild, wooly West. Us normal folks get a trifle bit anxious in situations like this."

"We'll have the drop on him, Cat, and I am armed."

"I tell you what, then. Why don't you let me have the gun? That would make me feel a lot better, sir."

Miles said, "You ever fired a gun before? Have you even had one in your hand?"

"Well … no. But how hard could it be?"

"Cat, if I gave you the Colt, you'd be more likely to accidentally shoot me than Manta. And besides, I'm a feeble old man, right? I need protection."

"I don't know about all that 'feeble' business. You got a few good licks in on that beast. And I'm pretty sure you could still whup most any fella you aimed to. Why—"

"Cat. You aren't getting the gun."

Cat pouted, jammed his hands in his pockets, and paced some more.

\* \* \*

The minutes stretched, the uneasy humor had disappeared. Miles sat stoically in the armchair and Cat had perched on the edge of the bed. They hadn't spoken for several minutes, only sat listening to the muted noise from outside and the less-muted noise from the adjoining rooms.

Gideon Miles knew how to wait with a focused mind. He'd lost count of how many rooms he'd waited in over the years, waited for fugitives from the law. He didn't daydream or get sleepy. All of his senses were tuned to his environment; he catalogued them all, noted small shifts in them, and waited.

Little Cat, on the other hand, wasn't used to waiting. He tapped his foot on the floor, tapped his fingers on his thigh, dreaded the coming encounter. He grew sleepy, then not sleepy. He thought about how fine some of Miss Tilly's whores looked. Then a sudden surge of terror would grip him as he remembered again why they were there.

When they heard Miss Tilly in the hallway, Little Cat jumped to his feet and Miles stood up slowly, pulling the Colt. Miss Tilly was talking, loudly, saying, "I'm sure

Celissa is going to be happy you asked for her. You are a big, strapping lad, aren't you?"

There was an edge to her voice, and Miles hoped the killer didn't notice. He motioned for Cat to move behind the big pine bureau before positioning himself behind the door.

The knob rattled and Miss Tilly said, "Go right on in, handsome."

In the limited confines of Celissa's room, Jimmy Manta seemed even larger than he'd been at the VioMiles. About six-four, Miles put him, and somewhere around 270 pounds. He wore a coat too heavy for the weather and a battered slouch hat. He strode right into the middle of the room before noticing the bed was empty and stopped.

Miles slammed the door shut with his boot and said, "Jimmy Manta. Put your hands up."

# Thirteen

Jimmy stared at the bed and smiled. Very slowly, he lifted his arms. Miles could see the outline of the axe under Jimmy's coat, nestled at his spine. It would be impossible for the killer to reach his weapon before catching a bullet in the gut.

Cat came out from behind the bureau, brandishing Miles's sturdy cane. To his credit, Miles thought he gave the appearance of fearlessness. And appearance was half the game.

Hands raised, Jimmy turned around to face Miles. "I didn't think you had it in you," he said. "I honestly thought you'd never be here."

"Sit down on the bed, Jimmy."

"Will you shoot me if I don't, Mr. Miles?"

"Yes."

Jimmy nodded. "I believe you would, sir. I really do. But it doesn't matter. I can't be killed. I am a Dark Spirit, Mr. Miles."

Miles said, "You're just a kid whose brain is rotting from syphilis."

"That's wrong. Did Mr. Carletti tell you that lie? He doesn't really know me. I am immortal. I am the Axeman."

Miles sighed. "No, Jimmy. You're a sick boy who killed a handful of defenseless girls. That doesn't make you the Axeman."

Jimmy snarled, "Those whores felt the kiss of steel from my axe. They had it coming. And only I could destroy them. You don't know any more than Mr. Carletti."

"You weren't even in New Orleans for almost half of the Axeman's murders. You'd lit out for New York by then, trying to find a daddy who'd abandoned you. But you were always fascinated by the Axeman, weren't you?"

Jimmy started to lower his hands. "I am a demon from your worst nightmares! I—"

"You're a killer, but you're not the same Axeman who terrorized this city before. You're a footnote. I don't know. Maybe you admired the real Axeman. Maybe you wished you had the freedom he had, or something. Or maybe it was just because he liked jazz music as much as you do."

"Shut up!"

"But you ain't him."

"I am! I am Darkness!"

"No. You slept with the wrong girl, got a dose, and went mad. You killed those poor girls because they looked like Celissa. You were rehearsing her murder."

"To Hell with you!"

Jimmy started to tear his coat off.

Miles thumbed back the hammer on the Colt. "I will shoot you, Jimmy."

Jimmy Manta threw the coat on the floor, started to reach for the axe tucked at the small of his back.

"Last chance, Jimmy," Miles said.

"You can't kill me!"

The axe was in his hands and he whirled on Cat, roaring. Cat looked startled that he'd become the center of attention.

Miles fired his gun, nailing Jimmy in the back.

The killer staggered forward a step, his roar stunted to a grunt. Cat brought the cane down hard on Jimmy's head, which the killer barely seemed to notice.

Still clutching the axe, Jimmy pivoted on stiffened legs, stunned eyes looking for Miles.

"Put it down," Miles said. It's not too—"

Jimmy's mouth twisted and he hoisted up the axe and lunged toward Miles faster than the former lawman would have thought possible. With the axe arcing toward his skull, Miles squeezed the Peacemaker's trigger again before pitching his head and shoulders to the right. The bullet grazed Jimmy's left shoulder and Miles felt the cold breath of steel sing past his cheek as the axe burrowed into the door.

Jimmy wailed in pain and frustration. Miles brought the Colt around for another shot but the killer was too close, looming huge in front of him.

"I'll kill you!" Jimmy screeched. He slammed his body into Miles, pinning the older man to the door. Miles felt his lungs expel air and tiny spots began to dance in his field of vision. While the killer tugged and pulled on the axe, trying to dislodge it from the door, Miles passed the Colt into his left hand and then flicked his right wrist, discharging the thin-bladed knife that had been sheathed along his forearm.

Jimmy freed the axe, stumbling back from the sudden release.

Miles slashed with the knife almost blindly. A deep, red furrow appeared just above Jimmy's eyes, and the killer screeched again, and his free hand clutched his face.

From behind, Cat swooped in and smashed a table lamp on Jimmy's head. Jimmy dropped to one knee but he immediately started to push himself back up using the axe for support, blood streaming down his face.

"Jimmy! Stop, Goddamn it!" Miles said.

"I'll kill you all," Jimmy slurred. "I'll kill ... I'll kill every human on earth ..."

Cursing again, Miles aimed the Colt center of mass and fired just as Jimmy surged to his feet.

Time ground to a standstill: Cat holding the lamp at the ready, Miles with the still-smoking Colt leveled, and Jimmy motionless and struck dumb. In the wake of the gunshots that had echoed through the small room, Miles couldn't hear anything except his own pounding heart.

Jimmy looked down at the blood spreading across his torso. The axe slipped out of his grasp and thudded on the floor. He looked back up at Miles with a question in his bloody eyes.

"I can't ... I can't die," he said.

Miles said nothing, but kept the Colt pointed at him.

Jimmy fell to his knees, then his hands. His breathing was rasping and harsh. He coughed up a gob of bright blood.

"I'm the Axeman," he moaned.

Miles holstered the gun, and Jimmy Manta fell on his face and didn't move.

* * *

Matranga showed up ten minutes later, with Antonio and two fresh goons in tow. Miles had checked Jimmy, found the killer was still alive—his breathing was shallow and his pulse weak, but the diseased boy clung to life.

Antonio strode up and kicked Jimmy in the head. "*Bastardo!*" he spat. "Filth!"

Miles said, "Knock it off."

Antonio started to argue, but Matranga put a restraining hand on his arm. Antonio backed off.

Cat had relaxed, assuming his usual smooth poise. He leaned against the wall, twirling Miles's cane, said, "There's your Axeman, Mr. Matranga. I bashed him in the head for you. Oh, and Mr. Miles put a couple bullets in him, just to make sure an' all."

Matranga wasn't amused. He glared at Cat, said to Miles, "Nice job. I'll deal with it from here."

The two new heavies moved to grab Jimmy's still body and lug him away.

Miles said, "Hold up. There's a few things you need to know."

"Mr. Miles," Matranga said. "I don't need to know anything about this punk. He's about to take up residence in the Gulf."

"You need to know his name."

"What the hell do I care what his name is?"

"He was born in New York City. Some, oh, twenty years ago. Around the time you were starting out there, Matranga."

"Miles, I don't—"

"His name is Jimmy Manta."

Matranga seemed to seize up. His body stiffened and his face went red. "What?"

Miles sat down in the armchair. He pulled his pipe out, tapped some tobacco into it. He was pleased to see that his hands were steady. He put a match to the pipe and sucked in the smoke.

"I talked to some of my contacts in New York today, Matranga. You had an alias in those days. They called you Charlie Manta, didn't they?"

Matranga choked, "I ... are you saying what I—"

"Meet your son."

Confusion ran rampant through Matranga's ranks. Miles sat back and smoked his pipe and waited them out.

Matranga squatted, gently lifted Jimmy's head and looked at his face. The gangster's expression was unreadable. Jimmy's eyelids fluttered.

"Goddamnit," Matranga said. "Goddamnit, anyway."

He stood up straight, barked, "Antonio. You and the boys get him to the hospital. Now. Take the auto."

"But, Mr. Matranga—"

"Do it."

"He killed Fredrico. And Petey."

"He's my son! Move!"

The thugs grumbled, but did as they were told. They hefted Jimmy up, and between the three of them were just able to carry him out.

Matranga sat heavily on the edge of the bed. He wouldn't look at Miles. He took a cigar out of his vest, eyed it blandly for a moment. Then he put it back. "You knew he was my son, but you shot him anyway."

"Yes."

"If he dies, I'll—"

"What? Exact revenge against me? I wasn't about to let him kill me or Cat."

"Goddamnit."

"For what it's worth," Miles said. "I hope he makes it."

Matranga sighed. "Yeah," he said. "Me too." He stood up, straightened his collar, and looked at Miles. "I'm a man of my word. I'll stay out of Storyville."

Miles nodded. "I'd expect nothing less from you … *Mr*. Matranga."

# Fourteen

There was nothing in the papers about Jimmy Manta or his relationship to Charlie Matranga. The murdered prostitutes were never mentioned, and life in Storyville lumbered along in all its depraved glory.

It was three weeks before Matranga came to see Miles at the club, shortly after closing time. They sat in the lounge, enjoying a drink, smoking, and Matranga told him about Jimmy.

"The boy's alive. But he's not long for this world. The syphilis, it's just eating away at his brain. I … I had him committed to the Alabama State Hospital for the Insane, in Tuscaloosa. They say he won't make it through the year. I was going to tell him, you know … that I'm his father. But I don't think he'd understand. He's too far gone."

Miles saw Matranga out, locked the door behind him. He leaned against it for a moment, pondering. Most of the lights were out in the VioMiles, and the stage, the bar, the extravagant furnishings were bathed in shadows.

He sighed. His thoughts turned to Celissa who died at Charity Hospital soon after the night Jimmy was shot. They told Miles there was a parade by the ward window at the time she died. A band outside played jazz music, but it's doubtful she even heard it.

Upstairs, Violet was still awake, reading in the sitting room. She smiled at him.

He said, "Violet. New Orleans is for the birds and I'm no club owner. There. I said it."

She cocked her head at him, still smiling. "As I recall," she said. "Wyoming is awful nice this time of year."

"Yeah. And Cash Laramie is still around there."

Violet laughed. "Oh, you boys. What are you going to do? Strap on your six-shooters and play lawman again?"

He laughed. "Nope. I'm a tired old man, remember? I need some rest. But Wyoming … Wyoming sounds damn good to me."

†

## About the Author

 Heath Lowrance is the author of the Gideon Miles adventure, "Miles to Little Ridge," as well as the novels *City of Heretics*, *The Bastard Hand*, and the weird Western collection (also from BEAT to a PULP) *Hawthorne: Tales Of A Weirder West*. He currently lives in Lansing, Michigan.

If you enjoyed reading "The Axeman of Storyville" featuring Gideon Miles, then you might also like the adventures of his partner, U.S. Marshal Cash Laramie, in the hardboiled Western novella "The Empty Badge" (from the short story collection *Trails of the Wild*) in the excerpt in the following pages.

ॐ

It's been weeks since Cash Laramie, the famed "Outlaw Marshal," has been heard from. Meanwhile, at the Federal Marshal headquarters in Cheyenne, Wyoming, some disturbing reports are starting to filter in about the notorious Driscoll Gang rapidly hitting a series of banks, allegedly with the aid of a badge-wearing accomplice claiming to be Laramie. Can it be true? Can it be that the lawman with the hair-trigger temper and the mile-wide independent streak has finally gone completely rogue?

The truth is seldom easy to find. And on the lonely, twisting trails of northwestern Wyoming in the 1880s, it was often lost forever. But every now and then, when those dusty trails converged in certain unexpected ways, answers were revealed and justice was delivered in a blaze of gunfire.

# THE EMPTY BADGE
*Wayne D. Dundee*

## PROLOGUE

The rain and darkness made it difficult for Cash to spot the sentry. In fact, he was almost on the verge of concluding that, because of the storm, the gang had decided not to post a lookout in the belief that no one was likely to be closing in on them under these conditions.

If they figured that, then they weren't reckoning on the tenacity of U.S. Deputy Marshal Cash Laramie.

At that moment, a rolling flicker of lightning coming quick on the heels of a low growl of thunder, reflected for the briefest second off the shift of a rifle barrel in some underbrush only a dozen or so yards ahead of where Cash knelt.

Cash backhanded rainwater away from his face and smiled grimly. With the lookout's position fixed firmly in his bearings now, he began to edge forward and slightly to the right. He moved in a low prowl, the barrel of his own Winchester Yellowboy pressed tight to his body, under the fall of his dull charcoal-colored slicker, so no sudden lightning pop could betray him in the same manner as the sentry.

The sound of his movement was effectively muffled by

the steady hiss of the falling rain and the low moan of the wind, not to mention the intermittent thunder. Even without these aids, however, Cash was highly skilled—thanks to the training he had gotten during his formative years being raised by a band of Arapaho—in the art of silently stalking prey.

As even the most fleeting memory of those years often did, tonight it caused Cash to reach involuntarily with his free hand and touch the arrowhead that hung around his neck on a leather thong. The arrowhead had been a gift from his dying Arapaho mother and he was never without it. Touching the simple talisman, no matter if done without conscious thought or awareness, somehow soothed and seemed to provide a measure of reassurance in the face of any situation.

Cash circled around to the rear of the lookout's position and then moved up behind him. Since making the costly mistake that gave away his position, the man had remained very still. But it was too late.

Gripping his Winchester in both hands—one near the end of the barrel, the other just behind the cocking lever—Cash leaned in close enough to smell the unwashed sourness of the man, even through the dousing rain. Bracing himself, he raised the Winchester up above the man's head and then lunged forward, sweeping the rifle down over the sentry's face and jerking back hard against his throat. Cash felt the windpipe collapse, heard the crunch of the larynx. The victim struggled briefly, one foot kicking in and out, hands clawing at the rifle, trying to pry it away. But it was all in vain. Soon his body sagged limp and still.

Cash let the body slip to the ground, and then he dropped

into a motionless crouch, listening intently, eyes slitted against the brilliance of the lighting pops while taking in as much as he could during those brief moments of illumination.

Satisfied the brief struggle had not been heard and was not generating any response, Cash rose up and stepped forward over the fallen body. He didn't know which member of the Driscoll gang he had just killed, but it really didn't matter. Unless, of course, it was Everett Driscoll himself. The elimination of their leader would have devastated the other gang members and made the rest of Cash's job a lot easier ... but that was too much to hope for. No way Everett was even-handed enough to assign himself sentry duty, especially not on a night like this.

Cash stepped out of the underbrush, out into the open and the rain again, and began making his way upslope toward the mouth of the shallow cave where the remaining four members of the gang were holed up for the night. He allowed himself neither remorse nor regret over the one he'd killed. Leaving the man alive—even unconscious and restrained, if he'd taken the time—was too much of a risk to have that close behind him while he went to deal with the others. Furthermore, there wasn't a member of the gang who hadn't proven many times over to be evil and bloodthirsty enough to deserve killing.

At the top of the slope, Cash paused to one side of the cave's narrow opening. Off to his left, where he had determined some time earlier the horses were staked, he heard one of the animals chuff. From inside the cave came so much ragged snoring it was a marvel any of those present could sleep a wink. And overhead, thunder growled regularly.

Cash smiled his grim smile again. Christ, with so much other noise drowning out his approach, it almost seemed like he could have thrown caution to the wind and marched in tooting a bugle and beating a drum. But approaching a potentially dangerous situation with caution was too ingrained in Cash, too much a part of him, to ever change. It was what had kept him alive this long in a profession where anything less could be permanently career and life ending.

Timing it not to be backlit by a burst of lightning while he was framed in the opening, Cash glided ghostlike into the cave and flattened himself against the rocky wall amidst a pool of dense shadows. The interior was predominantly dark and shadow-filled, but the softly glowing coals of a nearly dead fire gave off a faint reddish light.

As Cash's eyes adjusted, he could make out the four shapes of as many sleeping men. In the confined space, their snores were even louder. But outside the storm was intensifying, the accelerated claps of thunder and increasing howl of the wind doing their share to maintain command over the sounds of the night. Cash knew the gang members were weary, having ridden long and hard to try and stay ahead of him. So he expected their slumber to remain deep. But at the same time he wanted to make sure he took advantage while that was still the case.

Again moving ghostlike, Cash advanced on the glowing coals and picked up a pair of medium-sized branches from the nearby pile of firewood. He laid these carefully across the coals and then stepped back, pausing to make certain his movement hadn't disturbed anyone. When he was confident it hadn't, he moved again, this time to seize up three rifles and one discarded gun belt he spotted lying outside the bedrolls of the sleeping gang members. He knew there was bound to be more weapons *inside* the bedrolls, but getting rid of these would be a start. He carried the confiscated guns over to the cave opening and flung them out into the stormy night.

Then he stayed there, standing just within the cave's entrance, giving him the widest vantage point over both the interior and the sleeping men. When the time was right, he wanted everything and everybody well lighted and well within his range of vision. Quietly, he pulled four sets of handcuffs from a slicker pocket and let them dangle from his free hand, making sure the chains were not tangled.

The freshly-applied branches started to hiss and then crackle and then the first tiny flames started to lick up out of the coals. Cash waited with the patience of an Arapaho hunter.

Behind him, outside, the storm continued to grow stronger. Pitchforks of lightning stabbed the boiling sky, thunder crashed almost constantly, and the rain came down harder, blowing against his back and skimming across the hinges of his jaw. Rivulets of rainwater were now gushing down from the rim of the high, rocky cliff into whose face the cave opening was notched.

Cash flipped up the slicker's collar and continued to wait. The branches were starting to burn stronger and the interior of the cave was growing brighter. Another minute or two and the time would be right to roust this pack of rattlers, shoot any of them who weren't smart enough to see he had control over the situation, and then—

Without warning, a fat section of rock and mud and gravel tore away with a great growling, sucking sound from the cliff face directly above the cave opening where Cash stood. It tumbled down and partially into the notch right on top of him. Cash had no chance to react. He heard the strange noise and felt the crushing weight all in the same instant. The top of his head exploded with pain as a heavy rock within the falling mass slammed against his skull and when he opened his mouth to cry out it filled with mud and gravel. Then his ears filled, too, and the only sound he could hear after that was the scream coming from inside him.

Four riders sat their horses on the crown of a low hill overlooking a shallow valley. Down on the valley floor, the yellow-tinted lights of a small town were starting to blink on like swarming fireflies. The sun was less than an hour set and soon the rising moon and a blanket of stars in the cloudless sky would cast a bluish silver contrast to the pale gold of the town's lamps and lanterns.

"Well, there she sits, boys," drawled Everett Driscoll. "Yuba City—as fresh and innocent as a honeymoon bride, waitin' for us to come along and pluck her cherry."

The horsemen on either side of him guffawed obligingly.

Everett was a big, heavy-gutted man with weathered lines around his eyes and a puckered scar on his left cheek, partially covered by curly whiskers shot with flecks of gray. He cut his eyes over to the rider on his left, the youngest of the bunch. "How about it, kid? You ready to play your part?"

When Vint Brenner responded, his tone didn't sound quite as confident as his words. "Hell yeah, I'm ready. Can't hardly wait."

Everett eyed him. "Sure you ain't nervous?"

The kid—lean and handsome, clean-shaven, with dark hair and intelligent eyes set off by a glint of recklessness—managed a smile. But it, too, seemed a little uncertain. "If I am, it's only from being too close to this damn thing." He reached up and tapped the U.S. deputy marshal's badge worn on the front of his shirt. "I been too long on the dodge from anybody packin' one of these. I'm afraid havin' it pinned right next to my skin might cause my poor old unaccustomed body to break out in hives or boils or something."

Everett threw back his head and brayed with laughter. The other two men—Everett's brother Clem, and their cousin Burt Ketchel—joined in and stayed with it until Vint thought they sounded like three jackasses carrying on. He let his uncertain smile stay in place, but he didn't see where what he'd said had been so damn funny.

"Whoee, that was a good one," Everett gasped when he was finally done laughing. "Boy, I been runnin' from jaspers wearin' badges for more years than you been alive. If bein' too long on the dodge was cause enough for a body to break out in hives if'n they ever *did* get close to a badge, then I would be one big-ass pile of leaking sores right about now from just riding beside you."

"Same goes for the rest of us," Clem allowed. He was three years older than Everett, narrow-shouldered but also carrying too much gut, with eyes set too close above a pointy little nose and a scraggly walrus mustache. "Havin' that badge ain't nothing to be nervous or scared over. Not at all. Fact is, gettin' our hands on that piece of tin and then Everett comin' up with a plan on how to put it to use along with the other stuff we took off that law dog's body, well it could turn out to be the best stroke of luck we ever run across."

No sooner had he spoken those final words than Clem frowned, his expression looking like he'd bitten into something with an awful taste. He cut his eyes anxiously over to Burt Ketchel. "Aw, hell, Burt," he said. "I'm sorry for the way that might've sounded. I sure didn't mean that losin' your brother—not that part of it—was any kind of good luck."

Ketchel, a tall, gangly, towheaded specimen with a grotesquely large nose and a bobbing lump of an Adam's apple almost as big, returned Clem's anxious gaze with sad, earnest eyes. "That's all right, Clem," he replied, his voice a surprisingly deep rumble from within his scrawny neck. "I know you didn't mean it that way."

Brusquely, Everett said, "Okay. Now that we've made sure nobody's tender feelings have been bruised and the kid here has given us all a good laugh, it's time to get down to the business that brought us here."

He reached back into his saddlebags and withdrew a pair of handcuffs that he clamped onto his wrists, giving the appearance that his arms were fastened together in front of him. In truth, however, the cuffs had been carefully filed so that the locking prongs slid into place with a realistic click and even provided a bit of resistance when tugged at. But only a minimal amount. When jerked forcefully, the cuffs would pop open every time.

Clem and Burt each produced their own pair of cuffs and clamped them on. Theirs had been rigged the same as Everett's. Meanwhile, Vint climbed down from his saddle and tied the reins of the three men's horses together so that no single animal could break free and gallop away from of the rest. Then he swung back up onto his own mount.

"Okay, that should do it," Everett announced. "Time to take your prisoners on into town now, Vint-boy." Then, his mouth tilting into a lopsided grin, he added, "Excuse me … I mean, Marshal Laramie."

\* \* \*

"Sure sorry to drag you away from the supper table like I done, Sheriff," Vint Brenner was saying. "I was aiming to make it to town before sundown. But I guess I don't have to tell you that the country hereabouts can be a mite rugged. And it goes without sayin' that these hombres I'm herdin' weren't being overly cooperative."

"Don't you worry about it. Not one bit," replied Tom Weatherby, the sheriff of Yuba City. He was a bespectacled middle-aged man, average-sized, with bushy gray sideburns and a good start on a pot belly. "Any time I can lend a hand puttin' Everett Driscoll and his bloodthirsty pack behind bars—not to mention bein' a service to you, Marshal Laramie—ain't something I consider any kind of inconvenience. It's a damn pleasure!"

Vint was finally starting to relax. In fact, he felt downright calm. It was all he could do to keep a wide, smug smile from spreading across his face. But that, of course, would never do. It not only would run the risk of raising Sheriff Weatherby's suspicions, but acting too cocky was bound to earn the wrath of Everett later on.

Still, it was mighty damn slick how they were pulling this off. How *he* was successfully passing himself as Cash Laramie.

When Everett had first suggested the idea—after they'd partially dug the limp, crushed body of the real Laramie out from under the mud and rock slide and stripped it of its gun and badge and the rest, including locating the marshal's big pinto stallion staked nearby that stormy night—it sounded plumb loco. Leastways, it sure as hell had to Vint, who was the one tagged to take on the marshal's identity because he bore such a close resemblance.

The others took to the notion quick enough, but Vint wasn't so fast to buy in. Although he eventually had to pretend to be sold on it (after all, it wasn't smart to show too much resistance to one of Everett's ideas), he'd remained unsure right up to the minute they arrived at Weatherby's house, interrupting his supper, and the sheriff took to calling him "Marshal Laramie" without hesitation.

The sheriff was equally receptive to Vint's well-practiced spiel about capturing what was left of the notorious Driscoll gang—having had to dispatch two of them in the process, he'd explained—and needing a lock-up to hold them overnight so he could get some much-needed rest before continuing on with them to Cheyenne. Weatherby was all too willing to make a couple of his jail cells available, and even offered to provide a deputy to stand overnight guard on the outlaws so Vint could catch some proper sleep in a soft hotel room bed.

They were on their way to the jail now. Weatherby was walking along beside the horses, pointing the way, jabbering excitedly as they proceeded down the dusty street. Vint was mounted on Paint, the real Laramie's confiscated pinto, riding behind the still-handcuffed Everett and the others, wielding a shotgun to maintain the appearance of being ready to mow them down if they tried anything funny.

When they reached the sheriff's office and jail, Weatherby's deputy—a young fellow he called Sweeney—was there waiting for them. Weatherby had arranged for this by calling out a patron from inside a saloon they were passing and sending the man to fetch Sweeney, who was out making rounds.

"Got your message, Sheriff," Sweeney said now, by way of greeting. "I ran ahead and made sure the cells were ready and everything."

The lad gave the impression of being fairly new to the job, obviously green, eager as all hell to please.

Weatherby nodded approvingly. "Good. Now tie those horses to the hitch rail there and then go inside and stand ready while the marshal brings his prisoners in. Stay out of the way unless he asks something specific of you."

"Yes, sir."

Vint dismounted and then Everett, Clem, and Burt climbed down, their cuffs and chains rattling convincingly. Vint moved in close behind them, still brandishing the shotgun, and herded them into the jail. Weatherby, who had taken time to strap on a gun belt before leaving his house, walked at the fake marshal's side with his hand resting on the grip of his revolver. As soon as they were inside, Vint heeled the heavy door shut behind them.

"I'd suggest putting 'em two to a cell. Right back there," the sheriff said.

Vint nodded. "Good idea, sheriff … except for one thing."

"What's that?"

"This!" Vint said, pivoting and driving the butt of his shotgun hard and deep into the sheriff's gut. Weatherby emitted a wet gagging sound as he doubled sharply forward and sagged at the knees.

On the other side of the room, Deputy Sweeney took a step and blurted "Sheriff!" without even thinking to reach for the pistol holstered at his hip. As the prisoners shuffled in, Everett, the strongest member of the gang, had positioned himself nearest Sweeney. Now, popping the modified handcuff restraints with a single outward jerk of his arms, he let the movement carry him halfway around so that he blocked the startled lunge of the deputy. The young man's momentum carried him straight into Everett's waiting fists and the flurry of clubbing blows they eagerly delivered. Sweeney was driven back and down, knocked unconscious before he ever fully comprehended what was happening.

It was over as suddenly as it started. For a long second, the only sounds in the room were the tick of a clock on the wall and the low groans leaking out of Weatherby.

Then Everett turned back to face the others, a wide, rake-hell grin splitting the lower half of his face. "Didn't I tell you it would work slick as bear grease? Didn't I?" His eyes shone with excitement. "And you, Vint-boy, you did terrific! Holy shit, kid, you were so convincing you almost had *me* ready to believe you were Cash Laramie."

Clem and Burt joined in agreement and praise. Vint flushed with embarrassment, but was pleased to hear it all the same.

"Hang on, though. Let's not get too full of ourselves," Everett cautioned, his grin fading. "The job is only part way done, remember."

The others turned sober-faced as well.

Everett started snapping off orders. "Clem, find something to gag and hogtie this stringbean of a deputy, then drag him over and lock him in one of them cells ... Burt, help me get the sheriff back on his feet so's he can start to catch his breath and get his mind right for what's gonna come next and what more we'll be needin' from him if he wants to see the rest of it go with nobody gettin' serious hurt ... Vint, you keep your eyes peeled to make sure nothing is stirring out in the street."

* * *

"This is rather unusual, no doubt about it," Mordecai Croft commented for the third or fourth time as he fussed with the ring of keys to unlock the rear door of the Pioneer First Bank & Trust, where he presided as president. "But anything I can do to assist in the capture and incarceration of the Driscoll gang is purely my pleasure. What's more, you can't imagine how much relief and peace of mind it will bring—no longer having to worry that *my* bank might be the next one in line for those ruthless dogs to hit."

Croft got the door open and led the way into the rear office area of the bank where he promptly lighted a pair of lanterns and adjusted them to full illumination. He turned to the three men who had entered with him—a sullen, pinch-faced Sheriff Weatherby along with Vint and Everett, whom the sheriff had introduced, respectively, as "Federal Marshal Cash Laramie and his deputy."

The sheriff had shown up at Croft's house, accompanied by the two fake lawmen, a short time earlier. Another supper interrupted, another request made by the renowned "Cash Laramie" to impose on the bank president in the guise of aiding law and order.

Croft handed one of the lanterns to Weatherby. "How much money did you say was in there?" he asked, tipping his head to indicate the satchel Everett was carrying.

The bank president was a tall man, solid-looking across

the chest and shoulders, but with a weak chin and a pale, doughy face framed by skull-tight, slicked-down black hair.

"Reckon the sheriff don't know the answer to that," Vint was quick to reply, aiming a disarming smile at Croft after first slicing a hard-eyed warning glance in Weatherby's direction. The sheriff was managing to follow the instructions he'd been given, but wasn't doing a very good job of masking his reluctance and bitterness toward the situation. Vint was concerned his ill-concealed true feelings might show through to a point where he'd cause Croft to start smelling something fishy.

"You see," Vint continued, "the sheriff don't know how much is in that satchel because I never told him. Truth to tell, I don't know myself. I never got around to counting it."

Croft's eyebrows went up. "That makes you an even more amazing man than I've heard, Marshal Laramie. Very few individuals would have the willpower to resist examining the contents of that bag if they suspected it contained a significant amount."

Vint shrugged. "I don't know about that. All I know is that I haven't had a lot of time for counting, not since we took those Driscoll scoundrels *and* the bag into custody. But according to the posse members who rode with me and my deputy until they petered out and turned back, Driscoll and his bunch made off with over fifty grand from the Hopperville bank. Since we've been steppin' on their tails practically from the first, I don't see where they had much chance to get rid of any of it."

The dollar signs practically danced in Croft's eyes. "You mean you expect fifty thousand or more to still be in there?"

While Croft was staring greedily at the satchel, Vint

glanced again at Weatherby. Everett had stepped up close behind him and was hovering there in a silently menacing manner. The sheriff continued to look a little chalky-faced and nervous, but was fighting hard to put up a passable front.

Returning his attention to Croft, Vint said, "If that was the true start figure, then I guess I do. You can see why I'd like to have it locked away safe and secure in your bank vault overnight. With the sheriff here agreeing to hold our prisoners behind bars in his jail, and the money now in the capable hands of you and your bank—well, that'd give me and my deputy our first chance in quite a spell to catch a peaceful night's sleep. Can't tell you how grateful we'd be. Then, come tomorrow, we'll move on with our prisoners and the money and be out of your hair."

"Believe me, for reasons already stated, the gratitude would certainly cut both ways," Croft assured him. "Isn't that right, Sheriff?"

"Right," Weatherby muttered tersely.

Croft beamed a wide smile. "Enough talk, then. Let's find a spot to bed down that money so you gentlemen can seek out the same and get the peaceful night's sleep you so richly deserve."

Croft led the way deeper into the bank, passing behind a row of teller cages then over to a large vault sunken into an inner wall. The flickering lantern light cast shifting, often grotesquely shaped shadows as they moved along. Vint was glad to see that heavy shades had been pulled down over the westward-facing front windows.

Reaching the vault, Croft announced, "Rest assured, the Hopperville money will be quite secure here until you are ready to reclaim it tomorrow."

There was a moment of awkward hesitation as—without wanting to make the precaution appear too obvious—the bank president positioned his body in a manner meant to make sure the others were blocked from seeing the numbers he spun to open the combination lock on the vault door. Once the act was achieved, however, it took only a few seconds of whirring clicks before the heavy door was unlocked and Croft gave a tug on the latching lever to pull it open. Lantern light spilled in to reveal the neat rows of safety deposit boxes, trays of coins, and tidy stacks of paper money.

Everett spoke for the first time, saying, "You're pretty cocky about havin' a real secure set-up here, ain't you?"

Croft's scowl indicated he was somewhat offended by the tone of the question. "Most assuredly, sir."

"Well then," Everett drawled, reaching for his Colt in a smooth, almost casual manner, "how do you explain us bein' here to rob the joint and you standin' there holdin' the door wide open to accommodate us?"

Croft's expression melted into one of confusion and then alarm. His eyes shot first to Vint for an answer, but all he got in return was the sight of the masquerading marshal drawing the Colt and aiming it at him underneath a taunting smile.

When the bank man's gaze went to Weatherby, the sheriff's expression was one of pain and regret. "They got us cold, Mordecai," he said dully. "The Driscoll gang is in town right enough. Trouble is, they ain't behind bars in my jail. Part of 'em's standing right here before you—including Everett himself and the young pup pretending to be a federal marshal."

Croft looked stunned. "But how can that be? We've all heard descriptions of Cash Laramie … The arrowhead talisman he wears around his neck, the big pinto stallion like the one outside. To say nothing of the badge! I don't understand—"

"I don't know the whole of it," Weatherby interrupted him. "But what I do know is that another gang member has got Sweeney under the gun back at the jail and still another has gone to my house with orders to blast my wife at the first sign of trouble if I don't cooperate fully."

"And that's all anybody *needs* to know," Everett said harshly. "Was a time—and not so very long ago, as you're both damn well aware—me and my boys would have ridden into this piss puddle of a town, shot everything and everybody to hell, picked your bank clean and left a pile of dead bodies in our wake as we rode away. What we're trying here is a less rowdy way to go about it. You could say I'm startin' to tame down in my old age. Oh, you and your gobs of precious money will still end up parting ways, banker man, but as long as everybody is willing to cooperate—like the sheriff is smart enough to see—it can be done without all the shootin' and killin'."

"Says you," Croft sneered.

"Damned right, says me," Everett snarled right back. "And as long as me and my boys are the ones who've got the bulge on this thing, what I say is all that really matters."

"For Christ's sake, Mordecai, do as he says," Weatherby urged. "Didn't you hear what I said before? They've threatened to kill my Mary if there's any resistance. They know where you live, too. What makes you think your wife is any safer?"

Croft's face turned purple. "Why don't you put ideas in their heads, you cowering fool?"

"Knock it off, the both of you! You want to go at each other's throats, we'll be happy to lock you in the vault before we ride away and whoever finds you in the morning can decide who came out on top … if we leave you alive at all, that is!" Everett took the lantern from Croft and shoved the satchel at him. "Dump out the wadded newspaper and adobe bricks we stuffed in there—that's the big haul you've been drooling over, banker man. Then start replacing it with what's gonna be our *real* haul. I'll tell you when you got it full enough."

Vint motioned with his gun to get Weatherby's attention, then held out his free hand for the other lantern. "You better do the money-handlin', Sheriff. Mr. Banker might up and have a stroke on us if he has to be the one to actually fork over his precious bills."

"You have no worry as far as me having a stroke," Croft said through clenched teeth. "I have every intention of living long enough to one day see you thieving bastards hang!"

Sighing wearily, Everett reached out and calmly placed his lantern on a narrow shelf jutting out from the wall near where he stood. Then, with savage suddenness, he wheeled back and slammed the long barrel of his Colt to the side of Croft's face. The banker staggered away from the blow, arms flailing in an attempt to catch his balance. All he succeeded in doing was to upend one of the coin trays as he went down. He sprawled to the floor with coins spilling all around him and a bright red welt forming over his shattered cheekbone.

"Goddamn you!" Everett bellowed. "I told you we were trying to do this without the rough stuff. But that don't mean I *won't* resort to the old ways if you push me too far. You've done opened the vault, you dumb bastard. You lost the one sliver of an edge you might've had. Blowin' your brains out now won't cost me a damn thing but the price of a bullet."

"Don't shoot him. Don't kill him," Weatherby pleaded. "He'll cooperate from here out. I'll see to it he does."

The sheriff leaned over to give Croft a hand back to his feet.

"Leave him!" Everett ordered. "He put himself there, he can haul his own ass back up. And he'd better make it quick 'cause he's wore my patience about as thin as I'll allow."

Weatherby straightened back up. His eyes bounced back and forth the outlaw and the fallen man.

Croft, who had sprawled face down, put his palms flat on the floor and lifted his upper body, at the same time rolling onto his left hip. He groaned faintly, either from the effort or from the pain of his broken cheekbone that was inflamed and already beginning to swell.

"Come on. Move it. We ain't got all damn night!" barked Everett. "Didn't you hear me say I've about run out of—"

Suddenly, Croft gave a hard push with both hands. He rolled the rest of the way over onto his rump and leaned into an upright sitting position. At the same time, his right hand flashed across his chest and reached inside the left lapel of his coat. It jerked out a second later gripping a large bore over/under derringer.

"No!" Sheriff Weatherby tried to protest.

But it was too late to stop what Croft had set in motion.

The sheer boldness of his move—going for the derringer with two guns already drawn against him—damn near bought him enough time to get off at least one shot. But not quite. The unexpectedness of his desperate act froze Everett and Vint only a fraction of a second before their Colts roared simultaneously, spitting lead and clouds of rolling blue smoke. Four slugs ripped into the banker, knocking him back down from his sitting position and hammering him to the floor. The derringer flew from his hand and went skittering across the spilled coins as they were simultaneously painted with gushing blood.

Weatherby threw up his hands and cringed back against the stacks of bundled money. "Not me! Don't shoot me, I didn't do anything," he wailed.

"Well," said Everett, re-adjusting his aim. "Then maybe you should have, you lily-livered puke." And he emptied the rest of his cylinder on the sheriff.

Watching Weatherby's limp body slide slowly down to the floor, Vint matter-of-factly observed, "He's gettin' blood on some of the money."

"It'll still spend, don't worry about it," Everett replied as he punched the spent shells from his gun and began reloading. "Start stuffing that satchel. Pick around the bloody bills as best you can."

Emerging from his bedroll under the lead wagon, Frank Wizarious—better known throughout eastern Wyoming, western Nebraska, and parts of South Dakota as "Professor" Wizarious of the Wizarious Wonder Tonic Extravaganza—was immediately drawn by the welcome aroma of freshly brewed coffee. The scent wafted from a pot perched on the coals at the edge of a small fire crackling in the center of the camp.

Hitching up his suspenders and stamping his feet a couple more times to better secure the fit of his boots, Wizarious wasted no time heading straight for the pot. He was a tall, lanky man in his late forties with a purposeful stride and alert, intelligent eyes beneath a ledge of bristly, gray-shot brows and a headful of equally bristly brown hair also shot through with streaks of gray. His lankiness might have been mistaken for sparse physical strength if one failed to note the thickness of his wrists or the solid, rolling balance in the way he carried his long frame. Still, given that he was frequently seen in the company of the show's heavily-muscled strongman, he generally came across as looking scrawny, even to the most discerning eye.

An attractive young woman sat on a folding chair beside the fire, a cup of the pot's contents already in hand. She looked up at the sound of Wizarious' approach and greeted him with a bright smile. "Good morning, Uncle."

"Good morning indeed," he responded. Then, rummaging a tin cup from the box of eating utensils that sat on the ground nearby, he added, "Made all the more so, it appears, by an early spurt of ambition and domesticity on your part."

Seizing the coffee pot with the aid of a leather glove to shield against the heat of the handle, Beatrice Hale—who performed in her uncle's show as Beatrice Blaze, songstress and trick shot artist—poured some of the steaming brew into the cup Wizarious held out. "Much as I'd like to take credit for this 'spurt of domesticity,' as you put it," she said, "I'm afraid I cannot. You see, I rose only a few minutes ago myself. All of this was already completed—thanks to our new traveling companion."

"You mean Smitty?"

Beatrice topped off her own cup and then returned the pot to the coals. "I guess that's what you've taken to calling him. He doesn't seem to mind."

"No, he doesn't. In fact, like everything else we've done to accommodate him—and none of it has been all that extraordinary, I dare say—he seems deeply grateful. And, you've got to admit, being called 'Smitty' rather than 'Hey, you' would be preferable to most people."

"I suppose," Beatrice conceded.

"Where is he, by the way?"

Beatrice made a non-specific motion with her hand. "He went off to gather some more firewood and fetch water to fill the water barrel on the wagon."

After taking a sip from his cup, Wizarious commented admiringly, "He not only is an industrious fellow, he makes a damn fine pot of coffee."

"True. The only skills he seems to be lacking are in the memory department when it comes to his identity and whatever events brought on the predicament in which we found him."

"You continue to be suspicious of him, don't you?"

"I don't really want to be," Beatrice said, giving a faint head shake that caused her spill of long, pale gold hair to shimmer in the early morning light. "But I can't help it. What's more, I'm surprised that neither you nor Theron aren't equally so—especially Theron, who seldom trusts anybody about anything."

The object of that observation, Theron Tolos, a powerful Greek giant who'd made his way west all the way from New York City and now played his part in the Wizarious Extravaganza as the Hercules of the High Plains, was still asleep in his bedroll under the second wagon. Growing up in one of the city's roughest neighborhoods had made him guarded and mistrustful at an early age and neither were traits he was ready to give up, even though in the company of those he knew and felt comfortable with, he was the first to crack a joke or rumble with hearty laughter.

"But when he makes up his mind, Theron has a keen sense for reading people," Wizarious pointed out. "Maybe you'd do well to consider that *he* has relaxed his suspicion where Smitty is concerned."

Beatrice scowled, failing to look convinced.

"The man was nearly dead when we happened on him, drawn by the circling vultures," Wizarious went on. "The blows he suffered to the head and body from that rockslide he was practically buried under *would* have killed a lesser man. He was unconscious for three days and has now been up and about for only two. It's amazing he's functioning as well as he is. Why is it so hard to accept he came out of all that a bit muddled and disoriented?"

Beatrice's brilliant blue eyes flashed. "Because it seems too darn *convenient*, that's why."

"I don't even know what that is supposed to mean."

"It means what about the other things we spotted where we found him? The fresh grave nearby, the signs of several men and horses having stayed there in that cave whose opening was almost covered by the same rockslide that caught him? Why did they just ride away and leave him that way?"

"Obviously, they left him for dead."

"So they took time to bury one man, but not another? What does that tell you?"

"Maybe Smitty came along *after* the other men had left and was unfortunate enough to get caught by that rockslide when there was no one else around."

"So it was the rockslide that stripped him of his guns and hat and every scrap of identity? And what became of his horse?"

"After its rider was unresponsive for a long enough time, is it so surprising the horse might wander off? And not every man carries a handgun holstered on his hip, you know. There are such things as rifles and you usually find them in a saddle boot, which could be where Smitty left his when he went to check that cave." Wizarious shrugged. "Horse wanders off, gun wanders off with it."

"You've got all the answers, don't you?" Beatrice's tone was annoyed, but not really angry.

Her uncle smiled tolerantly. "I have some possible explanations, that's all. Ones that might make our Smitty something other than the mysterious desperado you seem to want to conjure up. There is a growing acceptance of a medical condition, for instance, called amnesia that can affect a person's memory after a shock to the system such as Smitty suffered."

"Then why have you been so reluctant to take him to a doctor?"

"Mainly because I doubt any of the doctors in these small communities out here on the frontier have sufficient knowledge or experience to be of much use treating—or even verifying—such a condition. Also, there is the matter of Smitty's privacy. Considering the circumstances in which we found him, I think it best *he* makes the decision on just how much he wants to solicit input from others."

Beatrice seized on this admission. "Aha! So I'm not the only one 'conjuring up' suspicions that his past might be somewhat checkered."

"No, but you're the only one who's already convinced yourself—and pre-convicted him, I might add—of that mere possibility."

"I'm simply making observations and attempting to draw some conclusions from them."

"Okay. How about if I've got an observation that you apparently missed?"

"Such as?"

"Remember the shirt Smitty was wearing when we found him? I asked you to wash it and see if there was any use left in it so he'd have something to put on when he regained consciousness?"

"It was nothing but rags. So torn and battered from the rockslide that it was useless as far as ever being worn again."

"Agreed. But before you tossed it in the rag bin, I noticed something. On the left side of the shirt's front, in the area just above the breast pocket, there was a spot of bright color that wasn't as faded from exposure as the rest of the shirt ... it was the size and roughly the shape of a typical lawman's badge. A marshal, say, or maybe a sheriff."

"Are you saying you think our Smitty may be a law officer of some kind?"

Wizarious shrugged again. "All I'm saying is if the shirt he was wearing belonged to him for any length of time—in other words, if he didn't buy it used or something—then the wear pattern on it looked to me like *somebody* who wore it also wore some kind of badge." Another flash of the tolerant smile. "That may not make Smitty as exciting as a desperado on the run, but I think it's a reasonable alternative at least worth considering. It also could fit with some of those curious things you mentioned about how and where we found him, and provides reason enough to continue giving him the benefit of the doubt while he's trying to get things sorted out in his head."

Beatrice's shoulders slumped. "Now I feel foolish."

"Nonsense," Wizarious told her. "Your suspicions may yet prove to have merit. Better to err on the side of caution than negligence. In the meantime, we'll continue to allow Smitty to travel with us while he's recuperating. During that time, we naturally will keep a close eye on him, but we'll do so with an open mind."

ෂාය

Continue reading "The Empty Badge" in the short story collection *TRAILS OF THE WILD: Seven Tales of the Old West*, available from BEAT to a PULP books (www.beattoapulp.com)

# Other titles from BEAT to a PULP

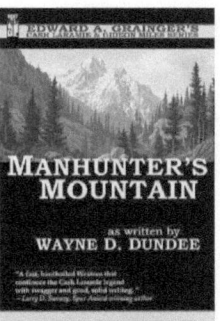

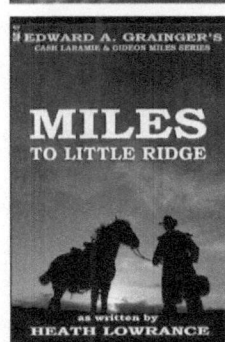
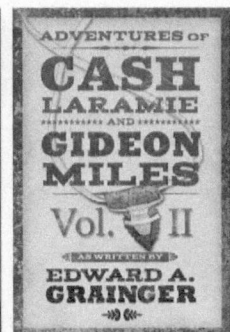

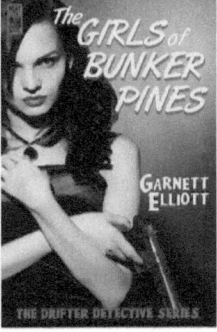
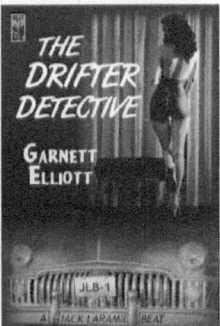

 BEAT to a PULP
PO Box 173
Freeville, New York 13068
USA
Email: btapzine@beattoapulp.com
Visit us at www.beattoapulp.com